The Illusive Diamond

by

Frank Wyndam

UPSO

THE ILLUSIVE DIAMOND

The Illusive Diamond © Copyright 2004 by Frank Wyndam

The author has asserted his right under the Copyright Designs and Patents Act 1988 to be identified as the author of this work.

All rights reserved. No part of this work may be reproduced or stored in an information retrieval system (other than for purposes of review) without prior written permission by the copyright holder.

A catalogue record of this book is available from the British Library

First Edition: June 2004

ISBN: 1-84375-097-X

This is a work of fiction. Names, characters, places and incidents are the product of the author's imagination or are used fictitiously, and any resemblance to any actual persons, living or dead, events, or locales is entirely coincidental.

To order additional copies of this book please visit:
http://www.upso.co.uk/frankwyndam

Published by: UPSO Ltd
5 Stirling Road, Castleham Business Park,
St Leonards-on-Sea, East Sussex TN38 9NW United Kingdom
Tel: 01424 853349 Fax: 0870 191 3991
Email: info@upso.co.uk   Web: http://www.upso.co.uk

CHAPTER 1

He laid in the ditch that he expected to become his grave. The bullet wound in his chest was hurting like hell and the pain in his frostbitten feet was getting worse causing him to squeeze his eyes shut.

He heard the crunching of footsteps in the icy snow and opened his eyes. An Indian face was looking down at him with a gun in his hand pointing at Simon's chest. The Indian face was joined by a second Indian face and the two stood motionless, looking down at him. They stood like statues seemingly unable to comprehend what they were looking at. They looked at him the way they might look at a wounded animal, in a matter of fact way. Were they considering the coup-de-gras?

It began snowing again and it occurred to Simon that he could be buried alive before they made up their minds to do something. He attempted communication.

'Can you take me to some shelter?' he squeaked weakly.

The Indians didn't hear him or didn't understand. It was likely that they didn't speak English. He was so cold now. The pain in his feet was creeping up his legs. He prayed that he could get them to understand him.

The Indian mind is not capable of working with probabilities. When involved in his daily work and the problem relates to his reindeer or his daily routine, he is very bright, but require him to change his priorities and he is totally incapable of making a decision.

Simon squeezed his eyes shut, partially in pain and partially in frustration. His biggest worry was wolves. They would attack reindeer but they seldom attacked humans, unless they smelt blood. Simon had an open wound and they might smell it when he was unconscious. He felt for his automatic for comfort. He had placed it on his stomach for easy reach in an emergency. Finding it still there he gained a confidence boost.

He opened his eyes again. One Indian face had gone but the first was still looking down at him. Presently, the second face appeared again and threw down a piece of dried fish, a bear skin and a water bottle.

Simon called with all the strength he could muster 'Will you get me out?' but they still didn't seem to hear. Both faces then disappeared.

After he'd been in the ditch a further twenty four hours he had become extremely cold and hungry. He felt for the automatic and took it in his hand. Pointing it upwards he pulled the trigger. Either he was too weak or the thing had seized with dampness. It wouldn't work. He buried it in his clothes to warm it up. He pulled the bearskin up over his face. As he tried to eat the last piece of fish the blizzard started.

He slipped into unconsciousness as his mind wandered over the events of the last few days. He remembered that Mark had an argument with a stranger. He had assumed that the argument was about the boundary or the position of the stakes. The other man had produced a gun when Simon had approached the two. Mark had lunged at the gun, took a bullet in the head and dropped like a stone. A second shot was aimed at Simon and caught him square in the middle of the chest throwing him backwards into the ditch. The last thing he saw was the stranger running towards his Range Rover.

He thought of Mark lying out there in the snow, possibly being ravaged by wolves. He hoped that the Indians would come back. It would relieve him of the worry of being eaten alive. It would also allow him to get Mark buried. He prayed that the Indians would remember to come back and he promised himself that he would bury Mark at the first opportunity whatever happened.

He pulled the bearskin further up again so that he was now completely covered and relatively warm. The blizzard had ceased now but it was snowing heavily. It occurred to Simon that the Indians could come back and not find him in the extra layer of snow and he could die of suffocation.

He'd eaten the fish, drunk some water and was feeling a little nourished. With the warmth of the bearskin he felt quite comfortable. It reminded him of the log fire in his sitting room and he questioned the reason for his being in the current situation.

CHAPTER 2

He'd been listening to a CD of Spanish guitar music as he checked the market prices. He put the paper down and walked over to the window. It was snowing again.

He pulled the heavy curtains, not to keep the heat in, he had triple glazing, but to shut out the scene. It looked very cold out there, probably ten below and he didn't want to be reminded.

As he moved over to the second window he noticed footprints in the snow. He remained still for a moment to see if the owner appeared. Whilst standing there he saw that the prints led to a bundle in the snow.

It appeared to be a body hunched up, just outside his boundary line about twenty five yards away. There was a patch of red adjacent to the body, which was in the foetal position.

Simon reached for the binoculars that he kept on a small table between the windows to identify birds. He zoomed in on the body. There was no movement and he was positive about the patch of red in the snow next to the body.

He grabbed the phone and dialled the emergency number.

A female voice answered with 'Fire, Police, Ambulance?'.

'I can see a body lying just outside my boundary' he explained.

'Name?' the officious voice asked.

'I don't know his name, he appears dead.'

'Your name Sir?'

'Simon Neufelt.'

'Address?'

'I don't know his address, I don't know the man at all.'

'Your address Sir.'

'212 Front Street, Potters Bar, Winnipeg.'
'What postcode is that Sir?'
'PB22. Look I just need somebody to take the poor chap away. He is nothing to do with me and he's just lying outside my house.'
'What is your Social Security number?'
'You're kidding. It's not me that's dead.'
'We have to be able to identify the caller Sir.'

He gave his Social Security number and the voice said that someone would be along in 30 minutes. He returned to the window and the binoculars and satisfied himself of his original sighting.

He moved to the next window and saw there was more than one set of prints but there was nobody making them.

He continued on across the hall to the kitchen. As he entered the kitchen there was a thump against the outside door. Someone or something had crashed against it. He turned the key and opened it. A clean shaven, well groomed man fell in and hit the floor gaping.

'Help me!'

Now it was Simon's turn to gasp.

It took Simon no more than five seconds to see the wound in the man's head, find some antiseptic and a cloth and set about bathing the wound, during which time the man had lost consciousness.

As he cleansed the wound Simon drew deep gasps of air through his teeth in complete sympathy with his patient as he knelt down beside him on the floor

There was a crunching sound of running feet in the snow outside and the door burst open. Looking down at the body on the floor an intoxicated Indian stood in the opening.

'Did he just come in?' he asked.

'Why, are you responsible for this wound?' Simon stood up and looked the Indian straight in the face.

The Indian became defensive.

'He ambushed me and took a swing at me with your pick axe handle. He missed and I took it away from him and gave him a taste of his own medicine. Then he staggered over here. Is he alive?'

'Just, no thanks to you.'

The Indian's eyes scanned the kitchen shelves and showed no concern for the wounded man.

'I'd get lost if I were you before I call the Police.' Simon wanted to get rid of him because he looked like trouble. At the mention of police the man was gone like the wind.

The snow was falling lightly over the wide open space that formed the view from the kitchen window. Everything out there was white, white and silent. The footprints were slowly disappearing now under the fresh fall.

In Canada huge distances exist between a house and its neighbour and the snow is seldom soiled by the soles of boots and remains pristine over great tracts of land. When footprints do occur away from pathways they tend to be treated with suspicion.

Simon stepped outside the kitchen door and looked for signs of the scuffle described by the Indian. The snow was disturbed over quite an area around the shed door and there were footprints to and from the shed.

He returned to the kitchen and looked down at his wounded visitor. He looked as if he was recovering. Simon made some weak tea and took some pain killers from the medicine cupboard with bandage and sticky tape. He went through to the kitchen to find the man had raised himself into a sitting position. Simon got him to his feet and walked him into the sitting room.

Sitting down heavily into an armchair the man introduced himself.

'My name is Mark Legat. I'm a geologist from Saskatchewan originally.'

'Where do you live now?' Simon asked as he dressed the wound on the head.

'We're neighbours' he said 'I live in my father's old house which is the next one to yours.'

'How did you run into Hiawatha?' Simon asked.

'I was skiing down to the general store when I broke a binding. I was just releasing both bindings when I saw him in the distance. He was heading this way and I thought it best that I should warn you. I know you haven't lived here long and it's best that you know about this character. Most of the Indians that come here from the north are harmless enough but this one is a madman. He's a drunkard and a killer. When he's seen, everyone locks their doors.

'I should warn you, he carries an automatic and he's served time for using it. I was the last person he shot.

'My head is clearing now. I can remember him clearly in the distance heading in my direction. At the same time I saw a man running up behind him. The second man appeared to strike the Indian. The two men exchanged blows and were waving their fists in the air.

'By this time I had arrived at your shed and I didn't see any more, but I heard what on reflection sounded like a pistol shot.

'I couldn't see what had happened but I wouldn't be surprised if the Indian shot the other man.

'Just before he shot me he had been attempting to break into an old lady's house and I had chased him away. He shot me as he was running away. I wouldn't be surprised if that is what happened here.'

'I wouldn't be surprised either' Simon said. 'I have what appears to be a dead body on my front boundary. I've phoned the Police. You have cleared up a potential puzzle. You can explain all this to them when they get here.'

As he spoke there was a knock at the door. Simon let the two policemen in and between them Simon and Mark explained the events that led up to the body on the boundary. The Police left.

Mark once again described the events of his previous meeting with the Indian and explained why a further meeting between the two would inevitably result in a confrontation.

'He'd put a slug in me and I was lucky he was a poor shot or he was intoxicated, as he is most of the time. I gave evidence against him and he swore he'd take better aim next time.

'He got three years for that and he's never forgotten it. It was only a flesh wound and I lived. I'd stopped him breaking into an old widow's house.

'When I saw him coming towards your house I tried to beat him to it to warn you but I only got as far as your shed. I took a swing at him with the pick axe handle in the shed but he got the better of me.'

Mark sipped the weak tea and swallowed the pain killers as Simon prepared some food. As they ate he insisted that Mark rest as long as he wished.

Eventually, they became firm friends and Simon told Mark that his surname was Neufeld and that he had moved to Winnipeg from Vancouver last month to see more of the country.

He was a Chartered Accountant, had been in banking all his life and was looking for a change in direction.

Mark described how he'd spent the last fifteen years mapping the great Arctic waste known as the North West Territories, the huge province half the size of Europe, and he had laid claim to a million acres.

The Illusive Diamond

Simon was enthralled with his stories of travel across the vast northern wilderness and how the frozen roads carve a pathway through the endless miles of forest of Spruce and Poplar. Mark explained how he spent less time up north lately and more time here in Winnipeg because he couldn't handle the cold for too long any more.

'I've staked out the acreage but the problem is that I can't register the whole claim right now because it will turn into a gold rush overnight.'

'You mean that you can prove the presence of gold?' asked Simon.

.No, I mean I can prove the presence of diamonds.'

'Diamonds? So why can't you register it then?'

'When I registered the Company five years ago, I included the current assets, which brought in such an amazing injection of cash that I haven't needed any increase in working capital since.'

'But that won't last forever.'

'Precisely. You see I have no interest in prospecting as such. My interest is in mapping the geology of the area.'

'So, for the last few years your company has been understating its true value. In the first place, that's illegal. In the second place your company could be taken over against your will' Simon stated.

'I realise that. That's why I'm concerned to update the registration quickly.'

'You're dealing with Vancouver Stock Exchange?' Simon asked.

'I'm bound to because of the high risk classification. London or New York wouldn't touch it. Vancouver specialises in this kind of business.'

Simon rubbed his chin thoughtfully.

'Mark, I do a lot of business with Amsterdam. Let me see what I can do.'

'That sounds a good idea.' Mark's face split into a huge smile.

'You understand that this is not a normal request.'

'I do and I appreciate your effort whatever the outcome.'

Simon walked over to the phone and dialled Amsterdam. He heard the clicks of the various connections and finally the Dutch operator spoke.

Simon initially spoke in Dutch, and Mark noticed that he asked for a female by name to whom he spoke English in a very friendly manner.

After a very lengthy conversation, he turned to face Mark.

'The situation is tenuous' he said 'since this is not their usual line of business. However they are happy to look at your registration documents to assess the worth of your company as a first step. They'll act only on my word so I'll need to survey your property first.

I'll book a flight to Saskatoon for tomorrow and a 'copter for the survey. We can be back in two days. Can you manage that?' asked Mark.

'I'll need you in Amsterdam. That'll be another two days after that, at least. I'll clear my diary for the next week.'

'Can I use the phone?' asked Mark 'I'll need to check on the flights before we do anything else'.

'Carry on' said Simon 'I'll be in my study. I have another phone line in there'.

Half an hour later Mark came into the study, his face noticeably happy.

'I've booked the planes for tomorrow. Is that OK?'

'That's fine' answered Simon 'you'll need to pack a bag. Take my skis and when you come back we'll eat. What time shall I book the morning cab for?'

'Eight' answered Mark and left.

Simon booked a cab and prepared a meal while he sunk a couple of beers, then packed a bag.

He returned to the study to check the share prices while he waited for Mark to come back.

A knock at the kitchen door broke Simon's concentration. He let Mark in and asked 'Mark, what's the name of your company?' as he walked back to the study.

'Legat Mining' called Mark from the kitchen as he took off his coat, hat and gloves. He put the skis back in the rack and followed Simon back to the study, dropping his suitcase in the hall on the way.

Simon greeted him with 'I see shares are quoted at ten cents'.

'That's correct. They've been at that level for so long that investors have lost interest. When I registered my acreage I included one diamond pipe which is all I had discovered then. I produced a 60 kilo sample of dirt which produced 60 small diamonds. As usual, soon that became public knowledge. Diamond pipes don't come in ones, they come in clusters, and when a single find is reported interest is renewed in the area, and everyone starts shipping stakes up there to claim a piece of ground. There are a of people up there who have spent a lifetime digging the frozen ground, only to find nothing. But if you're lucky, every hundred tons of dirt extracted will yield around eight grams of diamonds. Then all you do is keep pouring money in. My drill is

The Illusive Diamond

working 24 hours a day seven days a week but I can use another ten drills.'

Simon broke in at this point, 'Mark, how many pipes have you discovered?'.

'Twelve' came the answer.

'Twelve?' repeated Simon. 'You don't know if they're all producers.'

'I do. That's what I've been doing for the last five years. I've tested all of them. All I have to do is register them.'

'It'll be some time before you realise any money' Simon said. 'The best plan is for you to register your claim without wasting any more time. I'll attempt to raise some money and buy some shares in the Company as part of an ongoing plan to create working capital. I can understand your reticence to some extent Mark, but if someone makes a claim close to yours, starts work on it and discovers diamonds, there will be a rush to the area anyway, whether you like it or not.'

'That's true of course and your idea makes sense' Mark replied with no enthusiasm.

'I'm going to ring my broker before there's any movement in the shares' said Simon.

'That's wise because in two days' time after you've made your purchase the price will start going up.'

'OK' said Simon. 'Tomorrow we register your fresh claim. We go to Amsterdam with your paperwork and I arrange a loan. Then we fly up to your property.'

Simon phoned his broker and bought 5,000 shares in Legat Mining. Then poured two beers.

The room was filled with light during the day with tall windows that looked out over the vast snowscape reflecting the brilliant whiteness that was broken only by the occasional pine. The room was both a sitting room and library. Three walls were fitted with floor to ceiling bookshelves and the fourth was hung on either side of the grey stone fireplace with an elegant overmantle.

A wood fire crackled in the grate giving out a pleasant warmth and a welcome visual effect. There was a drum table in the centre of the room, its top laden with books.

Both men were seated in high green leather deep button chairs facing each other on opposite sides of the fireplace.

Simon broke the silence, 'I've decided that it's not worth you coming to Amsterdam with me initially. Why don't you go on up to the camp and I'll join you when I get back, if I'm successful. I'd prefer to be rejected alone.'

'That's fine' replied Mark laughing. 'I could use the time anyway.'

They resumed their drinking in silence until Simon went to the kitchen and brought back bread and cheese which they promptly did justice to, finally retiring around midnight.

CHAPTER 3

Mark was born in Saskatchewan and was taken south where his parents purchased a house, the house in which he lived at the moment. He attended University in Vancouver where he qualified in Geology. Then he joined his father prospecting in the North West Territories. When his father retired he began mapping the area alone.

After forty years his parents died. His father had little to show for a lifetime spent prospecting, except wounds from a couple of gun fights, but he was still healthy and in one piece when he died at ninety.

Both his parents were of Scottish descent and Mark inherited their dour Scottish personality. It was said that he had little or no sense of humour. He kept his own counsel, trusting no one else's judgement or opinion. He was now fifty years old and had been told by his doctor to slow down. He was ready to slow down, in fact he was ready for someone to take over the whole shooting match.

In the position in which he was qualified, his technical judgement was spectacular but running a business was not one of his qualities. He would like to get rid of the business end of the company, in fact he would like to rid himself of the whole company. It needed fresh blood, a fresh outlook. Simon could provide those qualities. His qualifications and experience made him ideal for the position of managing director. Simon had been placed on his path at the right time and he should take advantage of it.

They had decided that it would be pointless for both of them to go to Amsterdam. Simon would go alone. They changed the flight arrangements and telexed the new registration requirements to Mark's broker in Saskatchewan. Simon would join Mark up north on his return.

Simon's flight had been delayed by sixty five minutes. Sitting in the airport lounge he was reading last night's newspaper when he came across an article about a book entitled The Illusive Diamond written by a man called Mark Legat. The article described the author as the eminent geologist who had achieved considerable recognition since he published the book sixteen years ago, since when it had remained the most authoritative work on the subject. The author had spent most of his adult life in the diamond fields of Canada and had drawn the most comprehensive map of the North West Territory.

Simon dropped the paper into his lap and muttered 'Well, I never did. The man is amazing.'

When his flight was called he carefully folded the paper and slid it into his pocket as he made his way to the departure gate.

Climbing the steps of the 737 he realised he would not now arrive in Amsterdam until five minutes past ten instead of 9 a.m. He was pleased he hadn't arranged to meet her at the airport. He threw his briefcase into the overhead locker, unbuttoned his jacket and sat down heavily into his seat.

The stewardess was shaking his shoulder. He looked up.

'Will you check your safety belt Sir? We're coming in to land.'

'What happened to breakfast?'

'We don't wake passengers when they're asleep.'

He could do without the plastic bacon and the rubber egg but he could use a sweet black coffee.

The customary short screech as the wheels bit the concrete of Amsterdam runway and the plane taxied into the holding bay. Simon grabbed his hand baggage and joined the file into Passport Control.

Retrieving his single, medium sized suitcase he was ushered through Customs with no problems and into the reception area. As usual uniformed police were everywhere. Passing through the crowds he tried to pick out the plain clothes men, just for fun.

The cab reached the hotel in good time. He paid him off and went straight into a shopping mall. Wrestling with a large bouquet he entered the foyer of the hotel. Looking around he didn't see her at once. He looked around a second time and then he saw her. She was sitting in one of those big leather armchairs so typical of hotel reception areas.

The Illusive Diamond

Standing up she placed the magazine on the coffee table. As he came towards her she met his gaze, her mouth moist as she smiled.

The sunlight from the window behind her gave a mist-like quality to her silhouette. Her complexion was the colour of warm parchment, framed by golden blond hair.

Dropping his bag for a long moment they embraced. He gave her the flowers and whispered 'Why don't we take coffee in our room?'

'Sounds good to me' she said softly.

Picking up his bag they made their way over to the reception desk and then to the lifts.

They entered the room on the fifteenth floor. He dropped his bag, threw off his jacket and walked out on to the balcony. She picked up the phone and ordered the coffee.

From this height Amsterdam was spread out before him like a giant carpet, warmed by the red and gold of autumn before winter sets in and the biting north wind races through the canals.

He felt her arms encircle his waist and her head rested on his back as he leaned on the parapet. She joined him at the parapet and they watched the barges nosing their way laboriously through the ribbons of silver water.

Coffee and biscuits arrived and they chatted like a couple of kids as they munched and sipped. They showered and dressed in towelling robes and when he returned to the bedroom she had dropped her robe and was crawling into bed calling 'Come into bed Simon'.

He came over and sat on the side of the bed. He stroked her bare shoulders. She rested her cheek on his hand and her hand on his thigh. He slipped his robe off and climbed in beside her.

Simon had met Sarah six years before during one of his business trips to the merchant bank in Amsterdam where she worked. She'd been given his account to look after and they had become firm friends. The friendship had developed into genuine affection and they had become lovers three years ago. They shared a common interest in accountancy and the relationship had done her career no harm since she had risen to manager of her branch.

Simon asked if she had heard from his broker. She replied that she had and there would be no problem if he wanted a loan. He laid out details of the company registration and the newspaper report that he read this morning. Sarah was impressed and confirmed that there would be no problem with a loan especially in view of this added information.

The following morning he confirmed his flights to London then Saskatoon then on to Yellowknife. He sent a wire to Mark. Then he dropped her at the bank in his cab. He walked to the entrance with her as it started to rain. The rain dribbled over his face and down his shirtfront as he returned quickly to the waiting cab. She watched through the curtain of rain as he climbed into the back of the cab. She squinted through the splashes of rain on the glass doors of the entrance and wiped away the tears that filled her eyes. She wasn't sure how long it would be before she saw him. The Mercedes taxi pulled out into the traffic leaving dry lines of black asphalt as the rubber tyres squeezed a path through the wet road surface.

He dropped off in London to pay his respects to his bankers there and then returned to Heathrow in time for his departure to Winnipeg. Before leaving he phoned Winnipeg to confirm his connections to Saskatoon and Yellowknife.

When he arrived Mark was waiting at Yellowknife with a helicopter to take them up to the property. They landed a short distance from the work site and jumped into a Land Rover. Even at this distance he could hear the diesel engine of the drilling rig and when they arrived at the drilling area the noise was almost deafening. Everyone wore earmuffs. The drilling area was in a clearing in a forest. Simon glanced around the site as Mark pointed out the caravans scattered among the trees. He counted them. He was told that two were offices and the rest were living quarters. They stepped into one of the offices and Mark introduced the site manager Mac who poured some coffee.

Mark, leaning on a large map on the bench, proceeded to pinpoint the location of their whereabouts.

'This area is Echo Bay on the edge of Great Bear Lake where the Indians fish through holes in the ice. Our cook joins them twice a week to top up our food stocks.'

They all put on earmuffs which Mark handed out as he spoke. Mac was called over to the rig and Simon brought Mark up to date with the agreements in Amsterdam. Mark took Simon over to the caravan which he would share tonight.

He turned the heating up and said 'It gets very cold at night but during the day it gets as warm as five below on a good day'.

He woke to the music of the drilling rigs. The earplugs that he had pushed into his ears last night were effective but they had fallen out in

The Illusive Diamond

the dawn light. Apparently everyone used them. Mark was already up making coffee.

Simon showered quickly, dressed and poured himself a coffee. As they sipped the steaming liquid Mark said 'I thought I'd show you around the property today and talk about diamond mining'.

'Brilliant idea' Simon replied, thankful that he'd brought suitable clothes.

As they swooped around the area in the helicopter Mark pointed out how the perimeter was initially marked out, by throwing stakes out every two hundred metres, until the ground or time allowed the stakes to be driven in.

All the operators and technicians alike carried a tool that was a hammer with a spiked head and was used for instant appraisals of rock samples. When they landed from time to time Mark displayed its uses. He also showed how, in some places, a small explosive charge was required to break through the surface of the frozen ground.

From his perch in the helicopter, Simon could see mile after mile across the Keewatin tundra and endless lines of stakes that outlined the boundary of Mark's property and asked 'Are there any wild animals around here? I don't see any.'

'Plenty' answered Mark. 'In spite of the temperature up here there's an abundance of animals. There's Lynx, Mink, Marten, Beaver, Moose, Elk, Buffalo, Seals and if you're lucky you might see a White Fox. You've got to be very lucky because they move like a shadow and they are designed not to be seen. Their white fur makes them almost impossible to be seen. Once a year you see the Caribou gallop through. But no animals like the sound of the helicopter. They all disappear when they hear it coming. They stay away from the area near the rigs. You won't see many animals on the property, maybe just the occasional stray. If we were looking for them we would fly much higher and well away from the rigs.

'The Indians know where to look for them and they hunt well away from the property. They're a good bunch. All the men get on with them. Our mutual friend is not typical.'

'There can't be many Indians that live out here in this temperature' Simon queried.

'There are two tribes that inhabit the area. The Scarcee and the Chipewyan tribes. They have an abundance of small animals to live on and what they don't eat they trade at the store in Yellowknife or at our cookhouse. They are always looking for fruit and veg so we do lots of trade with them. They don't shoot the large animals because it's illegal but with such a selection of small animals to choose from there's no need. They catch the small ones in traps.'

They landed the chopper and Mark showed Simon a diamond pipe.

'How do you know that it is a diamond pipe?' Simon asked.

'Because of the presence of these minerals' Mark replied as he chopped away a piece of rock, and handed Simon a green crystal of chrome diopside and a red garnet. These are referred to as indicator minerals and where these are found, diamonds will be found.'

After spending the day inspecting the property they returned to the office where Mark produced some whiskey. Over a swig they planned to return to Winnipeg in the morning and work on the accounts. They threw their clothes into bags and prepared for an early start.

Leaving by helicopter at eight in the morning they were in Winnipeg for dinner that night eating a steak and sharing a bottle of French red at Simon's house.

'Mark, what was it that attracted you to prospecting?' asked Simon.

Mark took a sip of his coffee, then took paper and pencil from his pocket and began sketching as he started to speak.

'When you have read my book The Illusive Diamond you will see that I explain, the position of the indicator minerals is not exactly where the diamonds are found. I develop a theory that calculates the precise position of the diamonds in relation to the position of the indicators. If the indicators are found at a uniform depth then the diamonds would be found at a measured position from the indicators.

'You see, throughout history the whole area has been covered in ice. This ice has been continually on the move from east to west. As these early ice sheets moved across the landscape they carried with them the minerals of indication and by systematic sampling it is possible to trace the lines of the minerals back to the point from where they originally moved. That is where you will find the pipes.'

'How is a diamond pipe formed?' asked Simon.

'A pipe is formed by a volcanic explosion one hundred miles below the surface of the earth. Molten rock is forced upwards at astronomical speeds, cooling as it nears the surface. As it cools it takes on the structure of a rock known as Kimberlite. The pipe is actually a cone shape and it never occurs alone. They come in groups where the geological basement is weak, allowing the up-rush of lava. So if you find one, it is very likely you will find several more. In order to identify a potential pipe the top two metres of ground must be removed. That is where the initial investment lies.'

As he was speaking Mark had been making sketches. He pushed them over to Simon and explained each one.

'My initial interest in the area was never prospecting. My interest has always been in surveying, to prove a geological theory. My original idea was to draw up a mineral plan. I was never interested in prospecting as such. Ironically I can't prove my theory until I have uncovered diamonds in all the pipes I have identified and some pipes are richer than others.'

'I understand' Simon said.

'Diamonds are expensive because of the investment required. There are probably three thousand pipes in the world and only one per cent have sufficient diamonds to make mining worthwhile. The risk is so great that only forty pipes throughout the world have ever been mined and only ten are now in operation. The time period between initial sampling and identification through to actual profit can be twenty years.

'The weekly expenditure is unbelievable. Each drilling hand takes five thousand dollars a week. I'm at the end of my budget now Simon, I'm out of funds.'

'That's the price of secrecy' Simon said. 'However, I will provide a cash injection to maintain working capital and cash flow and in a few days we should have a different story. But first I have to have confirmation from Amsterdam.'

'Of course' Mark said.

Simon continued 'I'm expecting a letter from the bank in Amsterdam tomorrow. In the meantime we'll prepare a cash plan to cover all eventualities.'

'Excellent' said Mark.

Mark bid Simon goodnight, asked if he might borrow the skis again and made his way back to his own house. The snow was deep now and the snowploughs were out sucking up the snow and blowing it sideways into the air, where it came down in a shower to form large banks along each side of the road.

The moon cast narrow bands of light across the endless white space that continued forever northwards. The occasional poplar trees that had managed somehow to break through the rock hard ground stood like giant yachts painted white, in the brilliant moonlight.

He saw a light in his ground floor sitting room and slowed down. Was he seeing things? Did he leave the light on when he left? He reached his boundary fence and saw footprints in the snow. He followed them to his rear entrance, removed his skis and quietly opened the door. He stood still for a moment and listened.

He heard the distinct sound of someone rummaging through drawers. He followed the direction of the sound. He crept into the room and saw a man bent over his desk going through the drawers. Mark felt for his automatic and released the safety.

'Can I help you?' he asked. The stranger, shocked into submission, straightened up immediately. His hand went to his jacket pocket, the same as Mark's did. They both fired at once as Mark moved sideways. He went over to inspect the stranger who was lying dead on the floor with a hole in his chest.

Mark picked up the phone.

The police arrived in forty five minutes and immediately inspected the body.

'Yes' said the Inspector looking down at the face of the dead man. 'This chap is known to us. He's been in our care more than once. He's a two bit crook, a burglar well known in this area. Dangerous. He carries a pistol.'

'I know' said Mark. 'You should find a spent cartridge in that wall somewhere. The one he aimed at me.'

The Inspector picked up the phone and called his station. He asked for an ambulance, a photographer and a fingerprint man. He and his two policemen took measurements and made notes. It wasn't long before the photographer arrived and began his work. As he was completing, the ambulance arrived. They picked up the body and were gone in two minutes.

The police spent some time interviewing Mark and then they left. It was then that the shock of what had happened hit Mark and he felt drained. He downed a large Scotch and collapsed on the bed. He attempted to piece together the events of the last three hours. He could not believe it. His mind gave up and he fell asleep.

Simon, unaware of his colleague's experience, did exactly the same. But he was thinking of Sarah in Amsterdam.

It was seven in the morning in Amsterdam and Sarah was just bathing and preparing for work. She had a plan in mind that she intended to put into operation today. She had given the plan a great deal of consideration and she felt it was time to put it to the test.

The Illusive Diamond

Simon picked up the phone on the second ring. He was standing right next to it in the kitchen, making toast. Simon was shocked and visibly shaken when Mark described the happenings of the night before. Through the kitchen window he focused on the tool shed which was the scene of the Indian's last escapade.

Through the window he could see the distant mountain peaks which glistened white until the wind blew the snow off and then was replaced by further snowfalls. The air was full of snowflakes. For most of the year it was like this. The wind blew the snow off the mountains so that the air was seldom free of swirling crystals.

Simon asked 'How are you feeling Mark? Is there anything I can do? You must be pretty shaken up.'

'Oh I'm OK. I'll let you know if I need anything. I'll ring you later.'

They hung up.

Simon was as shaken up as Mark and his mind was totally preoccupied throughout the day with the thoughts of Mark blasting away at a stranger in his sitting room. Anyway the stranger deserved nothing less.

It wasn't long before the phone rang again. It was Mark to say that he was on his way over. He thought it was a good time to break a bottle. Shortly, the back door rattled with Mark's knocking. Simon let him in. He looked pale. Simon opened the first bottle.

Vitriano exhaled noisily between his teeth. Placing his fingers across his forehead he bowed his head, resting his elbows on the desk. His tight lips underlined his brooding cynicism.

He was lost without his Indian gofer. He had employed him for some time now and had come to rely on him. His last job was to watch the Legat house, identify Legat's movements and decide on the best time to go in.

At the right time he was to go in, search the place and bring back any paperwork appertaining to the Legat Mining Company. Also he was to search for and bring back a book called The Illusive Diamond. That mission proved successful except he couldn't find the book and Vitriano sent him on a further visit to return the duplicated paperwork and find the book.

He was usually dependable but having been asked to make this third visit he had not reported back. Perhaps he had been caught. If he had it would be most inconvenient. He would have to find another gofer.

Frank Wyndam

He paced the floor drawing deeply on his scented Russian cigarette. His heavily lidded eyes emphasised his brooding impassivity.

There was economy in his movement and his size gave him power. He had craggy good looks and there was an aura of rugged masculinity about him He was a worried man. If the Indian gave in under pressure and gave the police the name of his employer Vitriano was in real trouble.

CHAPTER 4

What brought Simon to his senses was a sudden rush of cold air. He opened his eyes to find his cover had gone and he was looking at clear sky. There was a sound of snorting and snuffling and a clanging of bells. The air seemed thick with a sickening acrid animal smell. The two Indians were standing over him talking in their strange language. They both bent down and picked him up bodily with no effort. He couldn't imagine what they intended. Slowly he looked around. It was then he understood. The barren snowfields which had been empty were now teeming with reindeer, milling around him. He was being moved to a sledge just two or three yards from his present position. They placed him on it gently, covered him up to his eyes in animal skins and lashed him down with rope. With a great effort he lifted his head and searched around the area for Mark's body, with no success. He decided that the Indians must have buried him. There was a jerk and the sledge began to move.

This whole process had happened so fast that Simon was disorientated. A few minutes ago he had been lying buried in the snow. Now he was being towed along the snow at an unsettling speed in the middle of a forest of running legs and nobody had uttered a word of explanation. The slats on the sledge began to rub into his back and he hoped the journey that was planned for him wasn't going to be too long.

Every so often they stopped and checked that he was still on the sledge and whilst they inspected his bindings he was surrounded with dozens of hairy noses sniffing around his face.

While they were stationary he raised his head and looked along his body and saw the hindquarters of the deer that was harnessed to the sledge. It was one of the bell deer and it was snorting and pawing the ground impatiently. When the sledge got under way again the bell around its neck would start clanging and the herd would fall in behind, padding along in the wake of the sledge in a narrow column four dozen strong.

The padding of hooves and the swish of the sledge runners became part of his new environment and somewhat alarming after the oppressive silence he had become used to over the last few days. When they stopped again he was given dried meat and some milk.

The wound in his chest was giving him no trouble and the pain in his foot had stopped, possibly because he was warmer now, in fact he was warmer now than he had been for some days.

As they swept along, he lay there eating his meat and drinking his milk and wondered what the plan was. Where were they taking him? With the clanging, swishing and padding and the gentle rhythm of the sledge his eyes closed, exasperated by the reflected brilliance of the snow that was so bright it could be seen through his covering and his eyes began to hurt.

He was weak and he could feel his remaining strength leaving him. He was induced to sleep, gladly surrendering, caring not whether he ever woke again.

As night drew in, the padding of feet eventually stopped. The straps of the leading animal were released and the animal was allowed to join his friends, who were making themselves comfortable on the ground, one by one, just where they happened to be standing.

Simon was given a piece of dried meat and some milk and another animal skin was thrown over him.

The Indians lay on the ground and covered themselves in skins looking much like the animals.

The temperature dropped drastically but Simon felt quite comfortable and slept well. In the morning he found that it had snowed during the night and everything was covered in a thick white blanket including the animals and the Indians.

Suddenly the Indians jumped to their feet and made a strange calling sound and all the animals stood, en masse, shaking themselves, and immediately started foraging.

Simon watched as selected animals were milked and he was given warm milk to drink and another hunk of meat.

The Illusive Diamond

The lead animal was hooked up and within ten minutes the column was off.

He settled down to the rhythm of the sleigh and was once again confronted with the powerful buttocks of the lead animal as it pressed its weight into the harness.

One Indian stood on the foot rail just beyond Simon's head and now and then, he would pick up the greasy animal smell from the man's feet.

They travelled through the night across miles of endless white landscape. He slept well and was woken by a blizzard as dawn was breaking. The blizzard became stronger by the minute and the Indians stopped the sledge. As they struggled through the wind the industry of the Indians indicated that urgent plans were afoot.

The sledge started moving again and the Indians and the animals with heads down fought the increasing strength of the wind and snow.

Eventually they arrived at a log cabin. The harnessed animal was disconnected and the two Indians manhandled the sledge with Simon on it into the cabin. They shuffled the sledge along one wall and fashioned a box to act as a bedside table and filled it with dried meat and plastic bottles of deer's milk.

With grunts and hand signals they indicated that they were going home to see the wife and kids during the storm and they would be back when the storm was over. They bid him goodbye, slammed the door shut and headed into the storm.

Simon felt thankful for the shelter of the cabin. In fact he felt warm and quite cosy compared to what it was like outside. He undid the straps that were holding him on the sledge and made himself generally comfortable. He loosened the skins that covered him to allow some air to circulate. Sitting up he took out some meat and milk and listened to the wind outside. He wondered how long his companions would be. He guessed some time tomorrow.

He wondered about Mark. Was he lying in a ditch somewhere as he had been?

That night he slept soundly, in fact it was the best night's sleep he'd had for a long time. He awoke feeling very bright and grateful to his Indian friends. He was surprised to hear that the blizzard was still blowing outside.

He drank some milk, ate meat and lay there listening to the wind. He began to hallucinate and for a time he saw Mark standing beside him and they had a lengthy conversation. He saw the shooting incident, not once but many times.

For one moment he thought he heard the Indians coming back, but it must have been a trick of the wind.

Suddenly, he was aware that the wind had stopped and it became deathly quiet. He lay there thinking for the rest of the day, wondering if he would ever get out of his predicament, eventually falling asleep.

He was awakened at daylight by the gentle movement of the sledge. The Indians were carefully dragging it outside. The animals appeared as they closed in around him, their wet noses snuffling over his face bringing him back to life. He was instantly reminded that he would never get used to their smell.

The animals crowded around him, giving the impression that they were very pleased to see him still alive. They were sniffling and dribbling and one actually licked his face.

Once again he was given fresh warm milk and more dried meat, then he was strapped in. Then they were off and not a word had been spoken.

The winter sun cast shadows in the indents left by the animals' feet in the fresh white snow creating a dappled effect on the huge dazzling surface. Simon hid his eyes under the covers to protect them from the glare.

The journey through the following day was much the same as preceding days. Boredom was setting in. He began to wonder how these people managed to survive this horrific lifestyle. They must be incredibly tough. His head continued to rock from side to side in the rhythm of the animals' feet. He shuffled his back to change position on the slats and reposition his mattress of animal skins.

At mid morning there was a stop for more milk and meat. His straps were checked and they were on their way again. The Indians seldom exchanged words apart from the occasional grunt. From his lofty position twelve inches above the ground Simon formed the impression that they appeared to enjoy a deep satisfaction in their lot and each was totally confident in his colleague who worked hand in glove with every movement.

As the afternoon wore on, darkness fell along with the temperature. The Indians appeared to be supping from a bottle of transparent liquid which Simon assumed was some kind of home brewed alcohol. This would prove to be the case as what Simon could see of their faces took on a warm glow which increased as the evening wore on.

When they stopped for the night they constructed a tent of animal skins and when they had completed the usual chores, they crawled in with a bottle each. After about thirty minutes they started chanting in a noise that sounded halfway between a dog howling and a cat crying.

His head ached and he closed his eyes. How much longer would he be on this sledge? The cold was beginning to get to his bones and he was becoming depressed. He began to think of Sarah. Would he ever see her again? Beautiful Sarah. Nature had created her in splendid proportions and she saw no reason to add to what she had been given by wearing jewellery or heavy make-up. She was just right.

Her hair was a kind of dusty yellow and in a certain light looked like gold cascading carelessly to her shoulders. Her nose was short and pointed and was designed especially for that face. Her skin was smooth and slightly tanned and was set off by that blue cotton dress she sometimes wore. Her beauty was not conventional but she was stunning in his eyes. Elegant and sophisticated, she didn't walk, she glided.

In business she commanded a great deal of respect for her opinions and her sharp analytical mind. She wasn't easily impressed. She was what every man dreamt of as the perfect woman. Would he ever see her again?

The sleigh rocked and bumped and he was brought suddenly back to reality. He pulled the cover from his face for some air. It was freezing out there. He saw the rear end of the animal pulling the sledge and decided that it was a ghastly sight. He pulled the cover over his eyes again.

Dusk was falling as he woke again and he thought he could hear a familiar sound. The sledge stopped and the harness animals were changed. He listened carefully. Yes! He heard it again. It was the sound of the diesel engine on the drill. When the wind changed direction the sound disappeared. They moved off again and he stayed alert, his ears tuned to the direction of the sound.

By the volume of the sound he estimated they were about two miles from the camp. As they swept along the sound got louder. He never thought that he would, one day, find that noise comforting. The countryside now included trees and as they drove along it became increasingly wooded. The herd dropped behind. They didn't like the noise. Pretty soon all the animals had disappeared except the harnessed one and he had to be led on.

They reached the clearing and the whine of the engine was loud. One of the Indians walked towards the collection of wooden shacks that stood amongst the trees. He'd obviously been here before because he recognised the words on the doors: TOILET and KITCHEN. He was heading for the caravan with the word OFFICE written on the door. Reaching it, he knocked respectfully. Mac's large frame filled the opening. The men recognised each other and Mac obviously understood the Indian tongue.

Within two seconds he was running towards the sledge. He pulled back the animal skin that covered Simon He recognised the face that was now waxen white, the sunken eyes, the receding cheeks. Simon looked up into Mac's big face and could see that he was shocked.

Mac ran back to the caravan and grabbed the phone. He dialled the flying ambulance then ran out to the sledge again taking a stretcher with him. He got the Indians to untie Simon, put him on the stretcher and carry him into his sleeping caravan and place him on the bed. They did this expertly.

Mac thanked them profusely and they left as quietly as they had arrived.

The helicopter arrived in forty five minutes and the two medics threw themselves into their work. They cleaned the wound in his chest and injected his frostbitten foot. He was carried expertly to the plane and placed carefully on a specially built bed and strapped in. Mac climbed into the state-of-the-art interior and sat beside Simon.

On the journey to hospital Simon explained what had happed. Mac was devastated. He sat and comforted Simon all the way to the hospital in Winnipeg where he was dealt with immediately. He sat in the waiting room desperately waiting for news from the operating theatre.

Eventually the trolley was wheeled out through the stainless steel doors and Mac stood and watched it head silently towards the recovery room.

A doctor came into the room and spoke quietly.

'Your colleague is safe and sound. The frostbite in his foot we have caught in time and this will heal. The wound in the chest was caused by a very small calibre bullet which fortunately struck the large button on his anorak. This was pushed into his chest and broke a rib. There is no other damage.

CHAPTER 5

The three weeks in hospital had passed very quickly. The police had been in to interview him and he'd answered all their questions and finally he'd been allowed home.

He'd been home less than an hour when the phone began ringing. It was Sarah.

'Where have you been for the last month?' she wanted to know. It took an hour to tell her and then she decided to come over to look after him. She would be there in twenty four hours. They hung up.

He began thinking about Mark and the business. He was sorry that he had offered to join the company. He now considered that it was more than a little hasty. He didn't need the stress and the worry, he was perfectly happy the way things were.

His light fair hair was sprouting grey streaks but his blue eyes which had become dull and lifeless in hospital had regained their customary healthy shine. In fact he was looking disgustingly healthy.

The phone buzzed.

'Sedgewick here' said a voice, 'of Sedgewick and Sedgewick, Accountants. We are accountants to Legat Mining. I just called to convey our condolences on Mr Legat's death and if there's anything we can do, please don't hesitate to ring.' He'd been notified of Simon's acquisition of shares in the company and repeated his offer to be available if needed. The only way he could shake off any relationship with the company was to sell his shares and walk away. Simon thanked him and hung up.

He thought of Mark. The ivory buttons on his corduroy jacket, the wide lapels. The cri-de-coeur of a man consigned to a career of interminable anonymity. Totally immersed in his chosen profession. His exquisite courtesy, his old world manners.

He was ruthless in this decision making with a surgical clarity for analysis. He had a piercing kind of intelligence which never ceased to amaze. His frayed cardigan and baggy tweeds presented him as a philosopher.

Simon was currently reading Mark's book The Illusive Diamond and decided it was a prerequisite for someone about to enter the industry, in fact he was immersed in it when the chimes of the front entrance brought him back to earth. He went to the door and threw it open. There she stood, framed by the dazzling white light that was the snow covered ground. Her green luminous eyes looking so deep and lovely.

She threw her arms around his neck, like a child, so pleased to see him. He paid off the cab and brought in her cases, the weight of which seemed to spell more than a week.

He led her into the sitting room then took her cases to the dressing room. She went to the bathroom whilst he made tea.

Over tea and biscuits he recounted the story in detail as she sat quietly and listened.

When he'd finished she said 'I just can't believe it. It sounds like a horror story. I just can not believe it.'

The bright morning sun had risen in a clear blue sky and it lit up the bedroom as he placed the cup of tea on the bedside table. She rolled over to face his direction and squeezed her eyes tighter before opening them. Her face shone like a child's. She ran her hand up the side of her face and back through her hair, holding her hand to her head, trying to waken herself from her dream world.

He watched the oval of her face. The top of her hair catching some of the filtered sunshine that came in through the lace curtains flecked with yellow.

'So, what are you going to do now?' her voice husky from sleep continued their conversation of last night as if they had never stopped.

'I'm not sure. I don't want to feel as if I'm taking advantage.'

The hushed intensity of his voice, the mixture of softness and strength that she found so comforting, was there, as he continued talking about the loss of his colleague. She could see that he was deeply affected by Mark's death.

She reached up and pulled his face down to hers. They kissed. Slowly

The Illusive Diamond

at first, then with hunger and desperation. When he slipped his hand down to her breast and further still, she tensed, and pulled herself closer.

Her voice was breathless as she whispered 'There's room for two'. And she pulled him onto the bed.

The phone rang. It was Sedgewick of the accountants.

'Mr Neufeld, further to my call of a few days ago. It appears that you are the only major shareholder in the company and therefore you will be required to take over the directorship of the company. There is also the question of assets. The house in which Mr Legat lived is company property and you may feel that it should be disposed of.'

Simon was flabbergasted.

'Just one moment Mr Sedgewick. I'm not ready for this. I'll need some time to consider this, is there anything else?'

'No that's it in a nutshell but my reason for ringing was to arrange a meeting to lay it all out before you. Why don't I ring you in the morning when you've had time to digest it. Then we'll arrange a meeting say for next week.'

'Fine' said Simon and hung up. He walked over to the window. He could not believe it. This whole thing was growing out of control.

An eagle swooped down to a rocky outcrop and grabbed something in its claws, returning to the blue sky yonder with no apparent effort whatsoever.

Sarah came over to him.

'What is it?' she asked. He explained what the accountant had said.

'Well what's so fishy about that?' she asked.

'Well where are the other directors for a start?'

'We'll make a list of queries to ask him in the morning.'

They walked to the town centre and visited a café overlooking the town square. It was cold and they were the only customers to sit outside beneath the awning. There was a big barbecue that people stood around waiting for snacks to be cooked before they wandered through the town chomping. They sat side by side facing the square drinking hot punch.

'I'll tell you what we'll do' said Simon. 'We'll fly over the camp by helicopter. You can see the whole camp from the air.'

'Fantastic!' she cried and leaned over and kissed him. They clung to each other cheek to cheek until ordering some kebabs which they munched hungrily and drank more punch.

As they walked back, hand in hand, Simon said 'While I was in hospital I had a dream that was quite frightening'.

'What was it about?'

'Well, in my dream I clearly shot the man who shot me. My gun was pressed against his chest and I fired six shots into him. He just laughed and turned away. When I was shot I landed in the ditch on my back and I saw him disappear into the snow. I have always assumed that he walked away, but since my dream it seems possible that I shot him.

'I remember having a gun in the ditch. Mark gave it to me as we left the office. It was a …', he stopped walking while he combed his memory. His eyes focused on a group of ducks riding the gentle swell of the river without moving, like ships at anchor. What the heck was that gun called? He raised his hand and gave a little start.

'It was a Glock something.' He began walking again. She slipped her arm into his. She could see he was deep in thought so she kept quiet. He was scraping the basement of his mind.

'I remember Mark saying 'Here, you take the 9mm Glock' just before we left the office. He checked the safety catch and filled it with ammunition. He even fired it into the ground so I know it worked. Yes that was it, it was a 9mm Glock. The funny thing is that it didn't work when I tried it in the trench, I suppose it was damp.'

They walked back in silence. He was happy that he was able to talk about his dream, she was happy that they were going to the camp and both were glowing with the effects of the punch.

When they arrived home he loaded logs onto the fire and they sat around it drinking, discussing what his approach should be to the accountants tomorrow.

He said 'My feelings are that I don't want to get involved with the running of the company and if I accept a directorship I will have to take some responsibility'.

The phone started ringing. It was the police. They had found two bodies near the western boundary of the Legat Mining Property and could he possibly assist in identification. Simon said he would visit the mortuary tomorrow. He phoned the airport and booked two seats for tomorrow to Yellowknife and a helicopter with a pilot from Yellowknife.

He turned to Sarah and said 'We're going to the camp tomorrow'.

They landed at Saskatoon airport at eight a.m. and took a cab to the police station. From there they were escorted to the mortuary. Sarah took a seat in the waiting room while Simon was taken downstairs to the cold storage area.

A trolley was wheeled out in front of him with the body of Mark whom he immediately recognised. When the second trolley was wheeled out, he was surprised to see that it was the body of the man who shot Mark. He looked at the name tag tied to the big toe. The name was Albert Shelby. It meant nothing to him.

They were escorted back to the police station where they were introduced to Chief Inspector Birch. They were given coffee in his very comfortable office and Birch asked Simon if he had identified the two bodies.

'Yes' said Simon 'I have identified the one name Shelby as the one who shot Legat, the man on the other trolley. I saw Shelby shoot Mark Legat.'

'Who shot Shelby?' asked Birch.

'I don't know. Shelby shot me one second after shooting Mark. I thought Shelby ran away.'

'Both bodies were found within close proximity to each other so Shelby didn't run anywhere.'

'I didn't know Shelby. I just recognised him as the man who shot me.'

'He was shot in the chest.'

'It couldn't have been by Mark. He didn't have time.'

'Were you carrying a gun on that day?'

'By sheer coincidence yes I was.'

'Why do you say, by sheer coincidence?' asked Birch.

'Because I have never before carried a gun and on that occasion Mark suggested I did' replied Simon.

'What caused the shooting to start?'

'Mark and I were carrying out a routine survey. We were marking out the positions for the boundary stakes. I was standing about 400 metres from Mark driving in a small pin on which to tie the line and Mark was holding the line at the point where the next stake was going in when a Land Rover drove up to Mark and Shelby jumped out.

'He walked over to Mark and began talking quite sociably at first but it gradually became heated and Shelby started raising his arms. I thought they were arguing about the position of the stakes. I finished what I was doing and walked up to where they were standing. As I approached Shelby took out a gun and started waving it about. I attempted to intervene and Shelby told me to buzz off and pointed the gun at me. Mark reached for the gun and Shelby pulled the trigger. Mark dropped like a stone. I felt a kick in the chest and I went down in the ditch. I must confess, my memory is not too clear at this point, but I had the impression that Shelby ran away …'

'What gun did you have in your possession at that time?' asked Birch looking down at the paperwork on his desk.

'A 9mm Glock' replied Simon.

Birch placed a bullet on the desk and allowed time for Simon to examine it.

'Would you allow us to examine your gun?'

'By all means' replied Simon.

'I'll arrange for someone to pick it up. I presume you haven't got it with you.'

'That's correct.'

'We found that bullet on site' Birch indicated the bullet on the desk 'but we could not find the bodies'.

Simon frowned. 'That's strange' he said.

Birch stood up and walked to the door.

'I appreciate you coming in to see us Mr Neufeld. Please keep in touch.'

Simon walked to the open door and stopped on the threshold. With a puzzled look on his face he said 'I don't know how Mark could possibly have shot Shelby'.

'You don't intend leaving the country I trust' Birch said as they shook hands.

'I may be required to visit Amsterdam in the next week or two.'

'Would you inform us if you do.'

'Of course.'

On the way back in the plane Simon said to Sarah 'It looks as if Mark may have shot Shelby'.

'Who's Shelby?'

'The man who shot me.'

Before returning home they hired a helicopter from Saskatoon airport and flew over the Legat Mining Property and Simon pointed out the ditch where he had lain for so long and the area were the shooting took place. He showed her the camp and the drilling area. They weren't able to talk much because of the noise of the engine but Sarah was thrilled by the experience.

After an hour or so of buzzing around and swooping up and down they returned to Saskatoon and took a plane back to Winnipeg. Sarah was full of excited chatter but Simon's mind was full of other things, for

The Illusive Diamond

instance, who shot Shelby. Someone must have shot him. It could only have been me.

His mind went back to the shooting. He remembered the Land Rover arriving. It drove up to Mark and turned in a semicircle to face the direction it had come from. Shelby jumped out and went straight over to Mark. But wait … ! He got out of the passenger side! Am I dreaming, thought Simon. Perhaps the vehicle was a left hand drive. He scratched his head. Am I beginning to talk in riddles, thought Simon.

The evening wore on and he decided to sleep on it. Which he did. But the night was not a dreamless sleep. He tossed and turned all night. The dream returned of Simon shooting Shelby in the chest. He woke up in a sweat.

He lay there thinking. He saw the Land Rover draw up. He saw it pull into a semicircle. He saw Shelby step out of the wrong side.

Simon phoned the accountants. He read over the list of queries he had prepared and then he asked 'Who are the other directors of the company?'

There was a shuffling of papers then Sedgewick answered 'Besides Mr Legat there are two other directors. Their names are P McPhereson and D Shelby.'

'D Shelby did you say?' Simon asked.

'That is correct Mr Neufeld. I have never met either gentleman. I understand the old Mr Shelby has become a little unstable in recent years.'

Somewhat shaken up, Simon arranged to see the accountants in a few days time and hung up.

Once again he tried to recreate in his mind the events leading up to the moment of Mark's death. He was under the impression that he saw Mark go for Shelby's gun. But at that moment he could have been holding his own gun. Simon couldn't have seen it because it would have been out of his line of sight. What was the gun that Shelby owned? The slug inside Mark's skull would answer that. And what was Shelby's christian name? Simon knew that the bullet in his own chest was a 9mm.

In the meantime he'd got some decisions to make regarding the Legat Mining Company. Did he or didn't he want to get involved with the company.

He phoned Mr Birch.

'Good Morning Mr Birch.'

Birch returned the greeting.

'Since our meeting I have spoken to the company accountants. It appears that there are two other directors Mr McPhereson and Mr Shelby. Would you know the initials of the man who was shot with Mr Legat?'

There was the sound of shuffling paper.

'Yes I do. The name was D Shelby. D for Dennis.'

'The other thing I want to ask you Mr Birch is what was the calibre of bullet you found in Mark Legat's head?'

'It was 9mm' replied Birch.

'So Mark was definitely shot by Shelby, as I was? But I don't believe that Mark shot Shelby. He just didn't have time.'

Simon and Sarah sat and pondered the question all day. How did Shelby get shot?

Was it Simon as he staggered backwards in a semiconscious state towards the ditch?

Was it Mark who shot simultaneously with Shelby?

Simon became increasingly worried. It was becoming more likely that he was the only possible killer.

He phoned Birch again.

'Mr Birch, I believe that I am the only person who could possibly have killed Shelby, even though I have no memory of it, since I was the only one there, there was no one else to do it.'

'That's circumstantial. It's not sufficient to hang you with' joked Birch. 'I'll need something more than that if you want me to arrest you. For instance, answer this question. Just before you hit the ditch, do you remember seeing the Land Rover?'

'Yes.'

'Well, when we found the bodies it had gone. The Indians reported the bodies but not the Land Rover. Either the vehicle was self propelled or there was another person.'

She was standing by the window in her dressing gown, deep in thought.

'I shall go for a run this morning' she said. 'I usually have a run every morning, but since I've been nursing you I've ignored my own needs.'

She turned and looked down at the bed. He was still buried deep in the bedclothes. She showered, climbed into her sweatshirt and trainers

The Illusive Diamond

and, leaning over the bed she kissed his forehead, the only flesh showing above the bedclothes.

'I shall be back within the hour' she called as she opened the bedroom door. As she went through the door, she stopped, turned and said 'Simon, remind me to call my office when I get back'.

As soon as she left the front entrance she started running, down the front path and out onto the road. She continued running and eventually came to the main street and the shops, which weren't open yet of course. She passed the café where they'd shared a barbecue and then she headed down the slope to the sandy shore and the lakeside.

It's funny, she thought, she'd never seen the steps that led down to the beach from the high street that Simon had mentioned. Perhaps they're further along, past the rock pile that formed the breakwater.

She planned to run as far as the rock pile then turn back.

She ran and thought of Simon, as she always did. She had definitely decided to marry him. She had decided to hand in her notice at the bank in Amsterdam and the flat where she lived and she would come to live in Canada.

She completed her run to the rocks and returned along the route she'd taken coming. Yes, she had made up her mind to leave Amsterdam. She was in love with this country.

She looked at the sky. It was becoming overcast and threatening. Snow was waiting to fall and it was becoming colder. There was the occasional break in the clouds where the sun forced through a shaft or orange light that beamed down onto the distant white landscape.

She was now back on the high street passing the greengrocer. He bid her good morning as he carried in a box of fresh cabbage from his van. She passed the newsagent whose door was partly open and she felt the blast of warm air as she passed.

It was now eight o'clock and she would be ready for breakfast when she got back. She wondered if Simon was up yet. She continued along the high street and looked at the hills on the other side of the lake. It was breathtaking. Yes, she was in love with this country.

Sarah's parents had emigrated from England to Nova Scotia where she was born and brought up and she had never tired of the rugged country. It had always appeared to her that this was a country that seemed to be waiting. Waiting for something to happen, in the vast, snow covered countryside. It was just waiting for somebody to start something, she never knew what that something was, just something. That's what gave it mystery and made it exciting.

CHAPTER 6

Jack Vitriano was the product of the Russian public school system and was regarded as an extremely bright student with a promising future. He qualified in all the socialist subjects including psychology, philosophy and economics. He studied a terribly capitalist subject, business administration, and surprised everyone with his grades, not least because so few of the masters knew anything about the subject.

A natural linguist he was fluent in most European languages, more than anyone else in the academy. He was without doubt an outstanding student.

During the cold war Russian agricultural planning suffered from a lack of interest because status hungry politicians could earn no points with their line bosses on such an unglamorous job. The result was that Russian agriculture suffered catastrophically. Wheat production collapsed to an all time low and stocks were non existent. Distribution ceased. Riots broke out in some towns and discussions were hurriedly organised within government departments.

Members of the foreign office were called to explore various possibilities, i.e. leaning on neighbouring countries. Vitriano was included in the team from the foreign office.

A proposal was tabled to apply to America for the purchase of some of their surplus stocks which they were known to possess. This was carried out and immediately refused by America who refused to do any business with Russia.

Vitriano proposed that Russia should send a team of buyers acting independently in the name of bogus companies with addresses in various countries around Europe. The scheme worked and shiploads of wheat were delivered via roundabout routes to be unloaded at suitable Russian ports.

The plan was a complete success and was not uncovered by the Americans for weeks. Vitriano was one of the buyers and the man leading the expedition. Needless to say all members of the team were English speakers.

The success of this operation took Vitriano to even greater heights, finally being sent to Canada to scout for geologists in the diamond industry and if necessary to buy up companies operating in the diamond fields. His country needed geologists specialising in diamonds. Russia badly needed to get a diamond industry up and running since finding that the country was rich in the resource but could not spare the time to train geologists and search for the stones, that could take twenty years. Russia needed to tap into this wealth lying in its earth.

Vitriano was the man chosen to carry out the Canadian operation and was given a work record to suit any enquiring businessmen. The whole team were given false names and passports including new nationalities. Vitriano's real name was Vitrianov.

Vitriano was attracted to politics which was very popular in Russia at the time. He studied the works of all the famous philosophers and discovered the difference between the philosophies held by the west and the east. The difference between capitalism and communism. He secretly came to appreciate that communism was outmoded as a political philosophy and that capitalism made more sense.

His interest in politics was recognised and when he was called up for military service he was made a political officer. During this period of his life he was stationed in and around the Russian satellite countries and army life gave him a new interest, shooting on the range. He found that shooting came quite naturally to him and he also discovered that he was a superb shot.

He remained fiercely patriotic during his travels and could drop into the local language and dialect quite easily. Dealing with local money changers he discovered the sharp practices that existed in the handling of currency and the laundering of money.

Over the years he became computer literate and studied the international markets. He discovered that dirty money moved across borders from west to east and back again and in fact all over the planet in the form of wire transfers. It was possible to launder money before it actually existed. This gave him a new dimension in his thinking.

Jack Vitriano picked up the phone.

'Central Police Station here' said a voice.

'What can I do for you?' asked Jack.

'We're just checking on a stolen vehicle' said the voice. 'My name is Stamford, Inspector Stamford. Do you own a Land Rover, Sir?'

'Yes' answered Jack.

'Have you reported it stolen recently?'

'No.'

'What colour is it?'

'A dark beige colour.'

'Thank you Sir. In order that I can discount your vehicle from our inquiries may I ask you one or two further questions?'

'Of course' answered Jack, now wondering what the hell this was really about.

'Has your vehicle been to the Great Bear Lake area recently?'

'No, definitely not' Jack was emphatic.

'Do you own a gun Sir?'

Jack felt that the answer to that was already known.

He answered 'Yes I do'.

'What make is it?'

'A 32 calibre Lugar.'

'Do you ever leave it in the glove compartment?'

'No, never.'

'Thank you for your time Sir, I'm sorry to have troubled you.'

Stamford reported to Birch.

She drew back the curtains in the sitting room. The sun was brilliant and it entered every room in the house, that was the reason she loved it.

It was beginning to snow outside, light snowflakes were blowing against the window in gusts.

She walked through to the kitchen where Simon was making coffee and toast.

She asked 'Why don't you take me up to the camp?'

'Because it's not the kind of place you need to go. It's very cold, very dull and very dangerous' he said seriously.

He looked up smiling. Her hair was exuberant and glossy. A kind of orange colour. She had a good figure in a light woollen suit, the skirt was knee length. Forty years old, she was not beautiful, not even pretty but surprisingly sexy. Good legs and a graceful walk, completed the picture of a very intelligent lady.

'To be honest I've no wish to return there myself. There's nothing attractive about the place unless you happen to have a love affair with diamonds and I definitely do not.'

He kissed her and returned to the toaster. She walked up behind him and put her arms around his waist.

'I don't have a love affair with them but I do think they're rather nice.'

'OK, we'll think about it' he said, turning and kissing her on the forehead. 'Now! Shall I show you the town?'

Neither of them was looking forward to Sarah leaving. Simon suggested that before she leave they spend two days in Banff skiing and visit Jasper National Park for a couple of days.

'You'll love it' he said. 'The lodge stands on the edge of a vast glacial lake ringed by the snow capped peaks of the Rockies. It's breathtaking' he said as he put his arm around her.

'If it's so nice, why haven't we been before?' she asked with a mock pout.

'It's also brimming with elk' he answered 'and it can be dangerous. I don't want you to get hurt.'

She put her arms around his neck and kissed him.

He booked two days in Jasper Park Lodge and two days in the Silver Springs Hotel in Banff. They packed a couple of suitcases, called a cab and they were off to the airport.

They landed at Calgary, hired a car and started a four hour drive to Jasper over a barren landscape that might have fallen off the moon. They passed Banff in a gentle snowstorm and saw a huge black bear strolling through the snow that stopped to watch them as they drove by.

They arrived at the lodge in time for dinner then sat on the veranda with their coffee and watched three bull elk indulge in a mating call that could best be described as a unified belch. It seemed as if the animals were putting on a display especially for them and they laughed happily until Sarah had tears running down her cheeks.

Simon was nervous. Everywhere he turned he seemed to turn into the path of big bull elks. Big bull elks were touchy in Northern Canada around that time of year. This is match making time and the elks consider that they have the right to wander the highways and byways the way that the cows do in India.

On their first day, they went out walking in Jasper National Park, one of the great scenic wonders of Canada. It was a perfect day and the air was champagne crisp, so pure it was positively intoxicating. It was an idyllic wilderness of towering pines, snow capped peaks and shimmering lakes. Until, that is, he walked into the orbit of a bull elk. The large, ominous creature with antlers was blocking his path.

The elk let out an enormous bellow. Simon heeded the warning and immediately backtracked. A fellow hiker who happened to be passing shouted a warning as the huge beast decided to attack.

Simon turned towards the thundering hooves and saw the animal charging at him, head down, antlers jutting forward, a fearsome sight. He jumped behind a large tree conveniently growing close by, already sheltering Sarah. The hiker went past him waving a walking stick and belted the hulk in the flank. The animal let out an enormous scream and took off.

There was a moment's silence as they all caught their breath.

'Phew' said Simon. 'Thanks' as he shook hands with the hiker.

'Never turn your back on them in the mating season' said the mature man with the walking stick. 'They killed 143 people in this park last year. They regard the park as their own.'

They spent two most enjoyable days in the park and Sarah was bubbling with excitement as they drove away. The route was a non stop sequence of craggy cliff tops. The only evidence of man's presence was the tarmacadam on which their wheels were rolling. It was a wilderness with mountains touching the sky and dense forests in which the horned mountain sheep meandered peacefully.

On the journey they came across a deep fissure in the earth over which a tiny footbridge had been suspended. They clutched the bridge's handrail as they peeped down into the bowels of the earth.

The light was now dusky, the shadows long and ominous. They were alone in what seemed the middle of nowhere. Sarah was in love with the place. She made a most profound statement.

She said 'Standing here in the centre of this grand stillness, one is suddenly aware of that most precious of commodities, silence'.

The journey down was two hundred miles and only one petrol station existed on the road.

They booked into the Silver Spring Hotel, showered and dressed for dinner. Over drinks Sarah said she was impressed with the hotel and she'd had a wonderful time on the slopes. During dinner on that last evening she said that she wasn't looking forward to going back to Amsterdam. In fact, she said, she had already made up her mind to stay for another week, as she brushed his cheek with the back of her hand.

The weather had remained pleasant and the snow crispy, ideal skiing weather. They had both fallen several times and laughed endlessly. They had stopped and sipped Glühwein and they had cuddled to keep warm. Sarah had whispered in his ear that she loved him and was thinking about moving in with him, leaving Amsterdam for good. What did he think of that?

Simon thought for one second and said 'I would be very happy with that but I would prefer that you make the decision and not me. It's a big step for a young lady to make, giving up her job and her flat on someone else's opinion. I'd love to have you here but I won't make the decision for you. You could easily get a job here with your qualifications and the people here are so nice.'

'I know' she said. 'I'm in love with one of them.'

They caught the plane at Calgary and flew back to Winnipeg.

Back at the house Simon busied himself warming the place up. He built a log fire in the sitting room while Sarah got out of her clothes and took a hot shower. After he got the fire going Sarah came in wrapped in a towelling robe.

Simon went in for a hot shower and when he returned she had prepared hot mince pies and tea.

They sat round the fire and munched and slurped. After a few minutes Simon turned and looked at Sarah and saw she had tears streaming down her cheeks.

He put his arm around her and whispered 'Why are you crying?'

'Because I'm so happy' she replied.

They curled up together and watched the flames dancing over the logs for a few minutes and then retired to bed.

It was not possible that Simon would ever have found the bodies of his friend Mark and the man Shelby in spite of diligent searching.

The site of the shooting was on top of a hill and when the two victims were shot they both fell down onto the sharp slope, rolling in different directions, sweeping piles of soft snow with them. Each came to rest some distance from the top in holes in the ground and were buried by subsequent snowfalls.

The snowflakes were falling in big white clusters, clinging together like a fairytale painting. Sarah sat in the window seat watching the snow settle on the lawn and saw it hanging from the trees like Spanish lace. It was so pretty. Everything was pretty here. It was a fairytale landscape and a fairytale town.

Sarah Watson was a bank manager. A girl who had graduated from university at the top of her class. Took a job in Nova Scotia and a rented flat next to the bank where she worked.

Ten years ago she took a job in Amsterdam and had never looked back. She became manager three years ago.

All her life she had kept herself fit. She had made a habit of running every day. Weekdays after work and weekends for two hours in the morning. She had been in Winnipeg for two weeks and had been running once. This morning she felt like running and it decided to snow.

She was forty and could pass for thirty. She attributed this youthful glow to her lifelong commitment to running.

As she watched, the snowfall subsided and eventually stopped. She showered and pulled on her sweatshirt, laced up her Nikes, tucked her hair under her hair band and crept into Simon who was still asleep in bed. She kissed him and outlined the route she would take. By eight a.m. she was running towards the outskirts of town and the lake. She felt good to be running after such a long lay off. Running in a fresh fall of snow was like running on another planet as she left her footprints in the virgin snow.

She thought of Simon. She loved him dearly and she missed him very much when they were apart, more so lately. She was seriously thinking of leaving Amsterdam and coming to live in Canada. He was a serious person and when they first met she thought that life with him would be dull, but it never had been, not for one moment. The opposite was true, life was exciting with him.

Her feeling for him had grown deeper over time and one might say that he was possibly taking her for granted. So what, she took him for granted. But she wanted to marry him. She was ready now. Yes, she was ready now. They weren't getting any younger and she wanted to have children at some time in her life and he was the man she would like to have them with. He was the man she would like to be the father of her children. Of that she was certain.

Yes, she was ready! She would go back to Amsterdam and ask for a transfer to a bank in Canada or give notice of her leaving the company.

She ran on, refreshed in the knowledge that she had made a decision. It was the correct one, of that she was sure and he was a decent and honest chap.

She ran with a new determination, a new defiance. In the vast expanse of sand the air was suddenly fresher and she breathed it deeply.

She was unaware of any movement or sound other than the sound of her own footsteps but instinct told her that she had company.

She arrived back at the house, perspiring, breathless and full of excitement. She showered and threw on a robe. Creeping into the bedroom she jumped onto the bed on top of Simon, bursting out the news of her decision, covering every detail of her plan to leave the bank and move to Canada, permanently. There was a grunt from under the covers but no movement. She collapsed in dismay.

'Simon, you're not listening to me' she pouted as she lay on her back talking to the ceiling. There was another grunt from under the covers.

She sprang up from the bed. Got dressed and swept into the kitchen to start breakfast. As she broke eggs into a bowl she suddenly stopped and looked out of the window. She saw a vision of herself in white wedding gown standing on the steps of a church. She sighed, then continued beating the eggs, singing gently to herself.

Suddenly, a pair of arms encircled her waist and Simon kissed the back of her neck.

'What was all the excitement about?' he mumbled into her neck.

'I just wanted to tell you of the decision I made whilst I was running.'

'Tell me again, I missed it.'

'I've decided to leave Amsterdam. I'm coming to live with you and work in Canada.'

'Fantastic!' he shouted as he picked her up by the waist and spun round in the middle of the kitchen. 'About time too' he shouted between her giggles and screams. Canada.

The following day she got up early again and slipped into her running gear. She felt good with herself. The world was at her feet. She was so happy she felt she could do anything.

She kissed Simon on his sleeping cheek and crept out of the bedroom door.
Then Simon called 'Sarah'.
She came back into the bedroom.
'Yes?'
'If you go all the way along the beach to the breakwater you could come up the steps that lead up to the high street and run back that way from the far end.'
'OK, I'll do that.'
She bent over, kissed him and left the room again.
She closed the front door quietly and began running immediately she hit the cold air. It was about a mile to the high street in town but it was a pleasant run and she enjoyed every minute of it. The landscape was magical. It was silent and white. :Pristine, unspoiled by man. She never tired of seeing it. She found it purifying. Just being here made one feel calmer. Every breath she took seemed to clean her lungs.

Soon she was entering the end of the high street. It wasn't exactly a prosperous street but it had its busy days. Mondays and Fridays usually. If she wanted bigger shops she would have to go into Winnipeg. Winnipeg was only a mile up the road anyway, but she was happy with this village.

It was Sunday and the town was still sleeping. Everywhere was quiet. The early morning snowfall had laid a carpet of white over the road and the pavement so that they appeared to be on one level.

None of the shops was open yet, including the café that overlooked the square where they had coffee. St Mary's catholic church was open, but it was open twenty four hours a day. No cars were on the street and there wasn't another person in sight.

The name of the village was Potters Bar. It was a suburb of Winnipeg and was a quiet little place. Sarah liked the slow pace of life here but sometimes the place seemed not merely asleep but dead.

As she ran down the main street in the winter sunshine she left footprints in the snow as her rubber soles picked up the fresh thin layer from this morning's fall. From one end of the town to the other she saw no movement other than her own. The only sound was the thump, thump of her rubber soled running shoes on the sidewalk paving and her laboured breathing.

She liked running in the morning, especially on these fresh, crisp, Canadian mornings. The temperature this morning was around five below but when you're running who notices. The sky seems bigger in the morning and things are brighter. Life is full of possibilities.

Now she reached the edge of the beach and sprinted over the sand to the water's edge. She ran along the firm damp sand at the edge of the lake scanning the distance for the breakwater where she would find the steps in the sea wall.

She felt wonderfully alive and felt a new spring in the soles of her shoes as she listened to the thump, thump rhythm of her running on the damp sand.

She was passing a rocky outcrop halfway between the high street and the waterline when she felt that she was under surveillance. She could see no movement but she was sure she was not alone. The only sound was the sound of her own footsteps, her heavy breathing and her own thudding heartbeat.

She stopped and scanned the vast expanse and saw nothing but the deserted sand and rock, a line of surf and thrusting rock formations breaking the surface of the sand and water that gave the foreground an exciting eye line.

Satisfied that her instinct was not reliable, she started off again, quickly finding her rhythm. Her trainers thudded on the firm sand and the breeze brushed her face and her hair and it made her feel good.

She ran on with a great feeling of satisfaction and a new feeling of excitement. In spite of the low temperature she was building up a sweat, she could feel the concentration under her arms and between her legs.

She'd gone about one hundred yards when she was attracted to a movement to her left among some loose rocks. She stopped and looked in that direction. Since the sighting was from the corner of her eye she had no idea what it was, but she expected it was a dog. But surely a dog would have come out to greet her.

She called 'Hello' expecting no answer, and got none.

She was curious rather than frightened. Standing there shining in perspiration, she kept running on the spot to maintain momentum and temperature.

She kept running on the spot and watched the rocks, expecting to see an animal jump out and sprint along the beach. When nothing moved she ran closer and around the rocks to take a closer look. Finding nothing of interest she shrugged and gave the rocks no further interest.

She was used to a somewhat sheltered life and that is why this town suited her. Aside from Mark's burglary and an occasional act of vandalism, which was usually the work of a drunken Indian, nothing much happened in this sleepy town. One didn't expect to meet real criminals until reaching the centre of Vancouver or maybe Amsterdam where she was quite used to reading news items of criminal behaviour. It was part of city life and that's where she was happy to leave it.

She left the rocks behind and decided that the movement she saw was imaginary. She was alone and that's how she liked it. She would run to the twenty foot high man made pile of boulders that formed the breakwater she could see in the distance and follow it back to the sea wall. Then she would return home.

That's what she did, taking a steady trot she returned home at a leisurely pace. She went straight to the fridge, poured herself a glass of orange and collapsed into an easy chair in the sitting room. Simon was still in bed. She picked up the book on the table beside her and scanned the title THE ILLUSIVE DIAMOND. She opened the cover and began reading.

Simon was born and grew up in Norway. His father was a self employed maker of skis and sledges. A lot of his time was spent walking through the forests selecting trees suitable for his work. He would take them back to his sawmill where he would store them until they were dry enough to work on.

He was a quiet man, working alone for most of his life he became something of a recluse. One doesn't meet many people in the dense forest of Norway just outside Lillehamer.

As Simon grew up he went to work with his father and accompanied him on his forays into the woods, and these were the happiest days of his life.

Eventually the family moved to Canada, to live just outside Vancouver and started Simon at school. Father found a workshop in a small town called Clinton in countryside not unlike the slopes and forests of Norway. There he set up in business.

Simon settled down at school and showed great promise. He passed the entrance examination into law school, finally entering a law practice in Vancouver where he lived and worked until his parents died. After spending some time winding up the estate he resigned from the practice and moved to Winnipeg. Sine then he'd been self employed working as a financial consultant, handling legal and financial affairs.

He enjoyed his life in Canada. It wasn't a lot different from what he remembered of his life in Norway. Canada had been kind to him and he regarded himself as a Canadian. His business was healthy and he'd got this house and he'd decorated it the way he wanted it. Life was good, he wanted for nothing.

He had no complaints and he was happy with his lot. Financially he was sound and he needed nothing.

He looked around the room, proud of what he was looking at. Yes, he was satisfied with what he'd got. If Sarah wanted to give up her job in Amsterdam and come to live in Canada with him that was OK. That would be no problem. Anyway he liked having her around. He was happy on his own but she was fun to be with. He smiled as he looked over at her sitting there reading.

He was amazed that she was so enthralled with THE ILLUSIVE DIAMOND. She'd had her face stuck in it for days. He knew she was a reader but he didn't think that she would be interested in that particular book. Anyway it kept her out of his way for a while.

The morning was bright and sunny and Sarah was feeling much the same. In fact she was feeling positively bubbly. They had made the decision. She would move in with him and he was as happy as she was. The next natural step of course was marriage. She was so lucky, how can a girl be so lucky. She felt as light as a feather this morning, her feet hardly touched the ground as she trotted along the dry earth of the forest floor.

Her new route would take her through the forest giving her a change of air and scene. In the distance she could see a mound built by the charcoal burners, smouldering gently. Not far from that was a huge pile of logs that she presumed were the fuel for the smouldering mound. It was high enough to be a danger. She thought that if the top log started to roll it might cause the others beneath it to roll, smashing anything or anyone it its path.

Arriving at the pile of logs, someone, a man, had climbed up to the top and was standing up there, hands on hips, staring down at her. For some inexplicable reason she was frightened. Tall and slim, legs apart, he exuded arrogance. They made eye contact. For a moment, staring directly up at him and the log he was standing on, she was transfixed. Looming above her, standing tall and motionless, he could have been a statue. But why should she feel afraid?

She wanted to turn and run but she couldn't move. She was frozen to the spot. Why? She'd never encountered this kind of fear before.

He was strange. His eyelids were heavy and he looked as if he came from another planet. His eyes had pupils that were fine like pinholes. He spoke unintelligibly. Was he foreign? His lips moved but she couldn't understand what he said. He seemed drunk.

She didn't want to appear rude but she felt she should leave now. Suddenly she didn't like the look of the man. On the one hand she was intrigued, on the other she felt that he was not in control of his behaviour. She thought he might be suffering the result of repressed emotions and should be pitied.

She thought he resembled a gas filled container with the lid pressed tightly down and might explode at any moment. He seemed to be under the influence of something, alcohol or drugs she thought.

She decided it was time to go. She thought that it was possible that the man was mad and a sensible woman would leave at once. She studied his face. He was positively different.

She was gripped in fear. The perspiration on her forehead became cold. The man's lips moved but she heard nothing. Was the top log about to move? She was suddenly aware of his teeth. Brilliantly white teeth in a deeply tanned face. He didn't seem real she thought.

Then in total control of every muscle of his body, he began to descend the log pile. Sure footed he moved at speed with no apparent effort. In seconds he would be beside her.

Suddenly, the trance was broken. She turned and ran. She wasted no time because he looked fit and she was sure she could be overtaken and attacked in the desolation of this wood with not a living soul in sight.

She felt that her experience in running was never needed more than it was now. She lowered her head and accelerated with every ounce of energy she could muster. She only had to make it to the High Street to be safe. She didn't believe the man would continue to pursue her once she reached there.

She had covered half the distance to the High Street and her confidence was growing. Then she turned and saw he was gaining on her. Fuelled by the fear that was growing inside her she attempted to pick up her pace, but so did he.

She began to whimper to herself as the High Street seemed to get farther away. It was so near and yet so far. She continued to the line of big cedars that she recognised from her entrance into the woods not so long ago. So big and dense were they that they hid the High Street from view and even reduced the daylight from that first part of the woods.

Her eyes, wide with terror, were fighting the perspiration that was filling them as she fought her way through the tangle of dense undergrowth that became thicker as she struggled through the trees slowing her progress. Should she turn and run straight at him and past him? she asked herself.

Evidently excited by the terror he had created in his quarry, like a wild animal he could smell fear and he was going in for the kill. He was gaining on her. Her heart was pounding fit to burst as the gap between them narrowed. She could hear him calling to her.

'Wait, I only want to speak to you. Why are you running away?' his speech was slurred.

Suddenly she was brought down in the undergrowth and he leapt on her. As she fell his weight pinned her down. His hands were all over her, touching her, tugging at her clothes. Her face was being pushed into the earth. She thrashed and kicked. The panic was real. She heard fabric tearing. The man was sitting on her tearing off her clothes scratching her back as he did so. She felt the hot touch of his flesh. He was pulling at her clothes as he stripped her. She attempted to shout but he pushed her face further into the earth. She couldn't breathe. She knew she was going to suffocate, there in the woods.

He had his way with her and left her naked, wedged in the roots of a cedar, dead, in broad daylight.

No shops opened their doors because it was Sunday and the town was preparing to go to church. There was no movement in the High Street, all was silent.

CHAPTER 7

After she had woken him he couldn't get back to sleep again. He'd heard her shut the door as she left. He thought of her. She was a pain in the rear at times. Her and her running. Every time he visited her in Amsterdam she would have to go running in the morning. She enjoyed it so leave her alone. She was a good girl really. Very capable and very intelligent.

He thought she was going to suggest marriage at any time now. If she did he would go along with it. She was no problem really. In fact she was good company, if he needed company. She'd be back soon. She was a happy girl. Nothing worried her. She was good fun to be with. Thinking about her he'd rather be with her than without her.

From his bed he could see the southern sky, brilliant orange in its morning colour. What a lovely morning. he must think about getting up now. Oh what a lovely morning. It was good to be alive on such a morning.

Perhaps they might go somewhere for a couple of days in the sun, before she went back to Amsterdam. They could both do with a bit of sunshine, it would do them both good. They could fly down to Florida or Mexico, just for a couple of days. He would suggest it when she came back from her run.

He raised himself from the bed and went in for a shower singing.
Oh what a beautiful morning
O what a beautiful day
Oh what a beautiful morning
Everything's going my way

He threw on a towelling robe and walked through into the kitchen. He poured two glasses of orange and looked at the clock.

She should be back any minute now he thought as he filled the kettle.

It occurred to him that he wasn't entirely happy about her giving up her job as bank manager. They would have to consider that before making the move. She was in an important position and highly respected. He didn't want her to ruin her life. He stood looking out of the window deep in thought as he sipped his orange. They had both lived alone for years now and there would be some bridges to cross.

She would have to take up some outside interest, a job of some sort. She might study the Indian language and become an interpreter. Brilliant! He laughed. She definitely would not be happy unless she was in some kind of business. He must come up with some ideas.

Where the heck was she? She'd been gone for almost two hours.

She would be coming in through the door at any minute now, laughing and breathless and looking for a glass of orange. He picked up the phone to check the availability of seats to Florida. Maybe they'd spend a week down there in the sun. After all she did say that she'd take another week. Yes! They had two seats available to Florida. Good. He'd surprise her!

He looked out of the window. It wasn't snowing, but the sun was out, it was still about freezing point though, not the kind of morning he would choose to go running.

She would need breakfast when she got back. He looked in the fridge. What would he cook for her? Yes, he had bacon, eggs, mushrooms. Good. He got them all out, ready to start cooking when she came through the door.

As he rattled around with pots and pans, humming to himself, he decided that he wouldn't mind being married. He had the feeling she would suggest it this morning.

They got the coffee started. It was time for her to return.

Another hour passed. Now he was worried. Where was she? She'd fallen over and couldn't get up. Perhaps he should go to look for her. What was the route she'd taken? He tried to remember what she'd told him as she was leaving. She was planning to run along the beach. That's it!

He decided to walk the route that he thought she'd taken. He pulled on his clothes and set off. He walked through the town, through the square up to the sea wall. Following the wall he scanned the beach looking down from up on the pavement.

He walked to the police station and reported her missing.

'She should have been back by nine, it's now twelve' he told the police.

'We'll ring if we hear anything' the desk sergeant said.

Simon had just reached home when the phone rang.

'I've just had a report of a girl's body in the woods.' It was the voice of the desk sergeant. Simon's blood ran cold.

He was in such a bad way that a police car came to pick him up and take him to the hospital where Sarah's body had been taken.

When they arrived, he was told that she had been confirmed dead and a list of her injuries was being prepared. He was taken down to the hospital morgue to identify the body. As he entered, the forensic technicians who were preparing the list of injuries, stood aside and Simon had an unimpeded view of the uncovered beautiful body. He collapsed, distraught.

A doctor was called and Simon was given an injection. He was carried up to a bed and hospitalised for twenty four hours.

Stamford picked up the internal and answered 'Stamford'.

'Morning Stamford.' It was the voice of the superintendent. 'Have you completed the report on Vitriano yet?'

'Yes Sir.'

'Then would you let me have it. Perhaps you would run through it with me?'

'Yes Sir. Right away Sir.'

Inspector Stamford was after promotion. There was a retirement coming up in his department. Chief Inspector Warren was sixty five in January and he was leaving at the end of the month. His job would suit nicely. Stamford had been an inspector for five years now and it was time to move on otherwise it would be time for him to retire before he got a department of his own. He was only forty nine at the moment and had passed all his grade exams.

He knocked on the super's door.

'Come in.'

Stamford approached the super's desk with the file proffered to the chief.

'That's all right, you run me through it.'

The super leaned back in the bo'sun's chair in readiness. The chair groaned.

'Well Sir. After investigating all those names on the list that you gave me, the only one to come up not smelling of roses was Vitriano. He's known to the San Francisco police department. They had him under investigation in nineteen eighty. He was found to be the top man when the Russians infiltrated the American wheat market. That was found to be a very smooth operation. The SFPD could find nothing that would stick so they allowed him to pass out of the country.

'Vitriano is a Russian national. His real name is Vassily Vitrianov. He is in this country to find geologists. Russia needs as many as she can get. They see it as a way of improving their balance of payments problem. The country is rich in minerals, diamonds and gold in particular, but they lack the resources and the brains to capitalise on that natural source of wealth. There's no time to train their own so they attract ours. They can use as many as they can get.

'Part of the grand plan was to purchase a small mining company in order to exploit the men and resources, shipping both to Russia whenever they are needed. Hence Legat Mining Co came into the picture.'

'Why didn't they go to somewhere like South Africa for the staff?' broke in the super.

'Because we have an abundance of the finest geologists in the world and we supply South Africa with them. The problem for Russia is that they need more than one or two, they need hundreds and need them now.

'Vitriano is so trusted that he's on an unlimited budget and his ultimate plan is to purchase the entire company whilst the shares are on the floor. It's the type of company that Vitriano's been searching for. The problem was that Legat was blocking the plan. Shelby was in his pocket but Legat didn't want to know. The Russian knew that Shelby was unstable and intended to dispose of him eventually. But it happened sooner than he planned. He intends to put Legat in the frame.

'Vitriano never left the Range Rover. When he saw the argument getting out of hand he pulled his handgun and took a bead on Legat, Shelby beat him to it and then blasted Simon. The Russian put one into Shelby as he turned and ran for the Range Rover. That's why Simon thought he was running away. It all happened in seconds. The Russian carries a Mark 5 Stechkin 9mm automatic pistol.'

The superintendent was speechless and very impressed.

'So what's our next step?' said the super.

'The next step, I suggest, should be made by the Russian, Sir.'

'Thank you Stamford, a brilliant report. Leave me with it, I'll get back to you.'

The superintendent started reading through the statement when the internal phone rang. He picked it up.

His secretary said 'I've the Winnipeg office on line one for you'.

'Put them through.'

'Hello Super, Muldoon here. I understand that you have a Simon Neufelt assisting in some inquiries?'

'That's correct Allan.'

'Well, I think you should know that we've just picked up a young woman's body from the woods that proved to be the body of the fiancée of Simon Neufelt. She'd been dead an hour when we picked her up and she'd been raped and beaten then suffocated. We've taken the body to the city morgue.'

'Thank you Allan, good of you to ring.' The super's brain started to buzz.

Lying in the hospital bed the ceiling gradually came into focus. The sedated state was receding. His brain was kicking into gear. The grey environment was becoming colourful. Suddenly he knew why he was here ......

He had to find the man responsible. To do that he had to get fit. He would start running every morning. He would take the route that she took. He would start shooting practice. He would spend every spare moment getting fit.

Now he was wide awake. Eyes bright and shining. He sat up and climbed out of bed, went to the wardrobe and got dressed. He made his way to the reception area and signed out. He thanked everyone, called a cab and went home.

He arrived home, made some food and sat down to think, to make his plans.

Tomorrow he would leave the house at seven in the morning and start running. He would do the same every morning and follow the same route. The route she took.

He would also join a gun club and practise some shooting. He must visit the mining camp and pay his respects. Perhaps he'd meet the Indians again. He'd like to thank them.

He went through to the study and checked the answer phone. Nothing of any importance. Wait! That was a peculiar accent. It sounded Russian. A number was left. Probably selling something.

He went in and finished his meal, sat back with the telephone book to find a shooting club.

CHAPTER 8

He poured himself another coffee and replaced the pot on its stand. Running his fingers through his blond hair he exhaled loudly. He had an aristocratic manner which was beginning to look weary.

The telephone buzzed suddenly and made him start. It was the police station.

'Muldoon here' a voice announced down the earpiece. 'It's regarding the man who was shot in the home of Mr Legat.'

'Yes?'

'Well Sir, we've arrived at the conclusion that he was working for a third party.'

'How do you arrive at that conclusion Mr Muldoon?'

'His pockets were full of mining company correspondence which he presumably was removing from the desk drawers when he was interrupted. He obviously was not interested in money on this occasion which is very suspicious for a man with his record. So we think he was working for someone else who was interested in Mark's company. Does that sound feasible to you?'

'Yes it does Mr Muldoon. With company correspondence in his pocket I can think of no other explanation. Would this have any connection with the shooting of Mark?

'I can't answer that at this stage, but we're in constant touch with our office in the Great Bear district and we'll uncover any connection.'

There was a pause, then Simon spoke.

'Mark's murder was probably a revenge killing. Perhaps the gunman had a brother.'

'With regard to our wider investigations in the area of Lake Rapids in Winnipeg, we interviewed a man who says he saw a man talking to a woman who could have been your fiancée at seven thirty that morning. Could you remember what she was wearing that morning?'

'Yes I can.'

'This man's account is so detailed that I think it's worthy of recognition, but at the same time, I don't want you to believe his story just for the sake of it.'

'OK, run it past me.'

'The man is a bird watcher and an artist. He was taking his dog along the tree line in the High Street. He was searching the trees with his new binoculars when he saw a young man standing on the log pile. He appeared to be in conversation with a young woman standing on the sand below him. She was dressed like a jogger. After a minute or two she ran back to the High Street.'

'Can I speak to him?'

'Yes, sure. I'll pick him up when it's convenient to him.'

'I'll be ready as soon as he is.'

'I'll arrange it and get back to you.'

At the arranged time Simon got to the police station and was introduced to the birdwatcher and Mr Muldoon whom he'd never met. The birdwatcher, Mr Johanson, had a pair of binoculars round his neck.

Simon was given a chair at the small table opposite Mr Johanson and immediately asked him to repeat his story, which he did in a most amiable manner.

Apparently, he was walking his dog, as he did every morning, leaving the house at 7 a.m. and returning around 7.45. First he walked along the edge of the lake to allow the dog to scratch in the sand, returning to the High Street via the stone steps which were built into the sea wall and could be easily missed. They were the only way up to the pavement and you might easily miss them. They should have been painted white for the old people to see. He walked along the pavement following the sea wall up to the forest then crossed the road, returning home on the opposite side of the street. It took the same time every morning.

That morning he took with him the binoculars that his wife gave him for his birthday the day before.

'I'm a birdwatcher you know' he said, as if by way of explanation.

Simon attempted to test him on his knowledge of birds.

'What birds does one see on the lake?'

'The Lapland Bunting, a brown sparrow sized little bird, along with its relative the Snow Bunting. They nest on the ground in the open tundra around the lake. They come at this time of the year from Greenland, Norway and Lapland, the region from which it gets its name. At this time of year it begins to grow fresh plumage which is in full colour in the spring and the male can be recognised by his chestnut nape and his call 'ticky-tick-teu'.

The policeman cleared this throat. 'What did you see with your binoculars?'

'As I was focusing on a bird in the distance, I was distracted by the figure of a slim man standing on the top of the log pile. I got the impression that he was posing, arrogantly like a defiant teenager. I thought it most strange at that time in the morning, so I zoomed in on him. I was immediately struck by the clarity of the lens. The face of the man was as clear as if he was standing next to me.'

'Can you describe the face?' Simon asked.

'Yes, I've already described it to the police and they've made a very accurate drawing of it.'

'Would you repeat it to me please?' Simon asked.

'By all means. The man had high cheekbones and flared nose, fiercely arching eyebrows with a full sensuous mouth and square jaw. His hair was of fine texture, the colour of straw. His neck was long and strong. His body was slim and muscled. The shoulders looked powerful, like an athlete's. He moved gracefully like a cat.

'There was a girl, a jogger, who had stopped to look up at him briefly. In one minute she turned and ran towards the High Street as he started to climb down the log pile. I turned and crossed the road at that point because the dog was pulling me to return home for his breakfast.'

Simon was silent. The blood drained from his face. This was a true account. He looked into the eyes of this man.

Johanson held out the binoculars and said 'Why don't you try them?'

Simon was choking. He couldn't answer. A cold draught passed over him.

He coughed and cleared his throat, asking 'Mr Johanson, do you remember what colour clothes the girl was wearing?'

'Clearly,' replied Johanson 'she had on a grey sweatsuit and white trainers and a white hair band'.

Simon felt as if he'd seen her ghost. There was a long silence.

The policeman held out his hand to Mr Johanson and said 'Thank you for your assistance. May we call you if we need your help again Mr Johanson?'

'By all means' Johanson replied, looking down sympathetically as he made his way to the door.

The police officer placed his hand on Simon's shoulder as he left Simon alone in the room for a moment. As he left he was given a copy of the drawing the police artist had made from Johanson's description. It was an amazing likeness.

The following morning Simon took a morning run, heading right up to the wood pile where he presumed she stood. It wasn't really a run, it was more like a plodding walk. There was nobody there. He followed the forest to the High Street and the sea wall turning left until he came to the steps. It was clear that Johanson was right, the steps could not easily be seen.

He had completed his planned distance and returned home.

The next day he visited the shooting club and took out a year's membership. He spent three hours there and was introduced to his instructor who in turn introduced him to a variety of pistols. Among the guns he handled was the 9mm Glock, the 38 calibre Smith & Wessen and the 50 calibre Desert Eagle. He was comfortable with all of them but found the Desert Eagle heavy. He shot a few rounds and the instructor said he looked perfectly at ease and was impressed with his handling ability.

Simon left the club feeling thoroughly satisfied as he bid the other members goodbye.

As he joined the fast lane on the highway, a vision of the man. The description that Johanson portrayed was so clear that Simon could see the man standing before him. He couldn't shake the picture from his mind. His future plan was clear. He was going to kill the man. Everything else was on hold. Johanson's description was so detailed it was incredible. What a memory that man must have.

That morning Simon had toured the route that Sarah had taken on that last day and had seen no-one. During his walk it occurred to him that he should take his camera and binoculars with him in future.

He took the slipway off the highway and entered the road leading to his house. Driving along the straight road he found himself studying the birds busying themselves in the snow covered fields.

He muttered to himself 'Today I have learnt a great deal' as he pulled onto his drive.

Simon phoned the company accountants and got a girl's voice.

'Hello, Simon Neufelt here, can I speak to Mr Sedgewick please?'

A male voice came on the line. 'Hello Mr Neufelt, Sedgewick speaking.'

'You phoned me yesterday Mr Sedgewick, what can I do for you?'

'Yes' said Sedgewick, 'have you reached a decision on the subject I referred to regarding your personal shareholding?'

'Yes I have. I've decided to take the directorship and if necessary I can fund any shortfall. But I cannot suggest a second director.'

'I may be able to help there' said Sedgewick. 'I've recently received an application for an upper management or executive position in any mining company for which we might be acting.'

'That sounds convenient' Simon cut in. 'What's his name?'

'Vitriano, Jack Vitriano' answered Sedgewick. 'His CV looks impressive.'

'Why don't you interview him for me and give me your impressions. Then I'll interview him.'

'A pleasure' said Sedgewick.

They said their goodbyes and hung up.

Simon poured himself a drink, loosened his jacket, sat down in an easy chair and breathed out heavily.

Simon had just returned from his run, made coffee and a sandwich and sat down deep in thought. Could it really be possible that the Indian burglar that broke into Mark's place was working for someone else? It stretched the imagination. He was just a small time bum. Perhaps he was working for a man who only employed bums. Simon laughed at his little joke.

In any case, who would be interested in company correspondence? He froze, the sandwich in mid journey towards his mouth. His eyes transfixed through the window, towards the shadows reaching down from the great trees in the distance. The company wouldn't be showing any great dividends at the moment ….. That's it, someone was shaping up to make a bid. The company could be picked up for peanuts at the moment. He reached for the phone.

'Mr Sedgewick, I have a feeling someone is about to make a bid for the company.'

He picked up his binoculars from the couch table and raised them to his eyes, focusing on the middle distance. He watched for a long time moving along the horizon, occasionally lowering them to rest his eyes. A strong breeze was buffeting in from the lake hurrying the clouds across the sky. In the distance he saw the flutter of tiny wings. He smiled to himself.

'I believe' he said to himself 'that I've seen my first Lapland Bunting'. Feeling exceedingly pleased with himself he returned to the telephone and Sedgewick.

CHAPTER 9

He was checking the share prices at his desk when the phone rang. He recognised the voice as one he'd heard on the answer phone, pleasant enough with an accent, Russian he suspected.

'I represent Shirnoff the famous Russian Vodka' said the voice. 'Petrov, Ivan Petrov is my name. I'm ringing to ask you to consider attending our function which we are holding at our country's Embassy. The reception is for company executives only and should you decide to attend I will be your personal host.'

Simon scratched his head for a second.

'What day is it?' he asked.

'Next Friday actually' answered Petrov in exaggerated English but with noticeable Russian accent.

'Yes I can make that. I'll be pleased to attend.'

'Fine, I'll drop you a card in the post and look forward to meeting you.' Petrov hung up.

Simon arrived at the Soviet Trade Mission, the biggest building in Regina Square at the time printed on the invitation. Russian flags adorned the front of the building along with vodka flags. He entered the reception area and handed in his invitation. He was shown into the exhibition area which was huge, and introduced to a salesman who immediately gave him a drink. There were dozens of representatives buzzing round trying to entertain everyone at once. He was engaged by his rep Petrov in shallow rep-speak as his eyes flitted round the room.

Suddenly, he focused on a face that he recognised, not from visual contact, but from the memory of verbal description. Simon dropped his glass. It was unbelievable. He'd never seen the face before but he knew every feature.

The face he saw on the other side of the room was the face described to him by the bird watcher at the police station. He recognised the high cheek bones, the eyes, the mouth. All the outstanding features that the birdwatcher had described were before him like a photograph. He was in shock. He heard the voice of Petrov.

'You dropped your glass Sir, can I refill it for you?'

'Er ... yes please Ivan.'

He regained his composure, excused himself and headed for the Gents.

For two or three moments he splashed his face. As he was drying himself in front of the mirror, a voice entered the room and went straight into a cubicle. The person to whom the voice was directed followed through the door and entered the second cubicle, speaking to the first man through the dividing partition.

Simon buried his face in the paper towel as he recognised the second man once again. He'd had a good look at the face and he was convinced that it was the man who killed Sarah. He lathered his hands again, searching for time. He needed time to think.

The first man left his cubicle and walked to the wash basin. Simon buried his own face in his towel again. The man reached for a paper towel, shouted towards the cubicles and left.

On the wall beside Simon was a roller towel. He tore the towel from the roller. He could see from where he was standing that the feet in the occupied cubicle were standing parallel to the door. He crept over to it.

With all his weight he threw his shoulder against the light door. The door swung open and the face he knew so well appeared before him. The needle was still in his vein, the strings twisted tight around his upper arm. His eyes were wide, the pupils pinpoints.

Simon threw the towel in his face and pulled the gun from his inside pocket. He stepped forward, pushing the man back into the cubicle. The man was struggling to remove the towel as he felt the pistol pressing against his groin. The towel fell from his face as he felt the bullet enter his crotch. His eyes were wide with shock and pain as Simon replaced the towel, stuffing the end in the man's mouth. The man's hands had gone to the source of the pain as Simon's face closed in on the man's ear.

'This, is for Sarah, the girl in the forest' he whispered between clenched teeth.

Placing the weapon under the trembling man's chin he quickly stepped back and pulled the trigger. Quietly closing the cubicle door he slipped his gun back into his inside pocket and left.

He passed out through the lobby and back into the exhibition room. Everyone was deep in conversation and the room was full of noise, clearly, no sound had been heard in here.

He helped himself to another drink as he was drawn into idle conversation with a representative. He was lecturing on the qualities of vodka, its lack of smell, its strengths and weaknesses, as he passed round the belushi caviar on a cheese biscuit. Simon didn't hear a word as he felt the heat of his hand gun against his ribcage. He finished his drink and left the premises and it started to snow.

As he walked out of town he felt as if a great weight had been lifted from his shoulders, he was thoroughly satisfied and even elated. He would have preferred the swine to have suffered a little more but it wasn't possible under the circumstances.

Feeling thoroughly satisfied he felt ten feet tall and a bounce had returned to his step.

He arrived home and poured himself a drink. Looking out of the window at the lightly falling snow he saw that everything was white as far as the eye could see and there were no footprints. He put on a John Williams CD and sat down by the fire.

The phone woke him this morning. It was Sedgewick the accountant to say that he hadn't heard from the man Vitriano with whom he had an appointment two days ago. He had phoned his number two or three times with no success. He would continue to try. Simon thanked him and hung up.

In the kitchen he made coffee and toast. He knew he would never meet Vitriano but he couldn't tell Sedgewick that. He finished his coffee and went through to the bathroom. He showered and dressed and went to the study.

Around mid-afternoon the phone shook him from his concentration.

'Hello, Muldoon here, of the Winnipeg police.'

'Hello' said Simon.

'I thought you'd like to know that a body was found shot at the Russian Embassy building last night. We were called in at one a.m. when the body was found. I see by the visitors book that you were there last night.'

'Yes I was invited by the vodka people who held a reception there. Terribly boring. Why did you think I might like to know? I have no interest in Russians.'

'Because he answers the description of the man we're looking for in connection with the death of your partner.'

'What?' said Simon.

'The description given us by the birdwatcher Mr Johanson matches the features of the face on the body we found last night.' Muldoon continued 'A car in the car park was registered to the deceased, Mr Manawa. The licence in the car included a photograph of Mr Manawa, an Indian.'

'Excellent!' shouted Simon. 'We have the man at last. How strange he should be at the Russian Embassy.'

'It's not that strange,' Muldoon was running his finger down a list of names, 'I have in front of me the guest list and it appears that everyone in town was there last night. He was very well dressed and the car was a Cadillac. I imagine he mixed with some high level business people.'

'It's good of you to ring Mr Muldoon' said Simon, 'if there's anything I can do to help please don't hesitate to contact me.'

It occurred to Simon that the police would ask to inspect his pistol. He took the gun from the desk drawer and placed it on top of the desk. He spread a clean cloth on the desk top and placed the gun on it. He stripped the gun down and removed the firing pin. With a piece of emery paper he rubbed down the leading edge of the pin and reassembled the gun.

With the gun in his pocket he drove to the gun club. After spending half an hour practising with his own pistol he stripped it down, cleaned it, and reassembled it again. He returned home picking up a takeaway on route.

Jack Vitriano was going through the papers on his desk. He had decided to acquire shares in one of a short list of four companies he had prepared. Of the four companies the Legat Company seemed the most promising. He had investigated all four companies and the Legat firm seemed ideal for his intentions. The company was short of money due to short-sighted management. The site manager was apparently a mature qualified geologist that was all he wanted.

The Illusive Diamond

The other companies were either too rich, too big or top heavy with management or staff, or both, for his purposes. He separated the Legat company papers and flicked through them. They were photocopies of papers the Indian had lifted from the files in Legat's study. He was an idiot to get himself shot by Legat in his latest visit. That was too bad. He'd soon find another gofer. Anyway, he'd now have no Legat or Shelby to worry about. He picked up the phone and punched in the number of his broker.

'I want to purchase every available share in Legat Mining. Ring me as soon as you've completed.'

He hung up and cleared his desk. He would wait for the return call and then ring Sedgewick.

Thirty minutes passed and the phone buzzed.

'Hello Mr Vitriano, Jacobs here at the brokers. I've picked up all available shares and you are now the major shareholder in Legat Mining Company. It happens that the Managing Director has passed away and his shares are floating so we were able to pick them up. He owned fifty one per cent of the stock.'

'Who are the other stockholders?'

'No one of any consequence.'

There as a shuffling of papers at the other end.

'Except for a Mr Thomas McPhereson and a Mr Neufelt.'

'Thank you Mr Jacobs. I'll be in touch.'

Jack put the phone down and immediately dialled the Legat accountants.

'Hello Mr Sedgewick, Vitriano here. I have to apologise for not contacting you earlier. Unfortunately I've had a death in my family and we are quite disorientated. May I ask when it would be convenient for me to call on you?'

'Good to hear from you Mr Vitriano. You can come in tomorrow if you wish.' Sedgewick was keen to get the matter dealt with. 'Ten in the morning would be fine.'

'Thank you. I'll come in at that time. Goodbye for now.'

Jack Vitriano sat back with a satisfied smile on his face. He had taken over the company!

Superintendent Birch picked up the internal and spoke to his secretary 'Phone Mr Neufelt and get him down here, would you?'

It had been established that Legat, Neufelt and Shelby had all been shot with 9mm shells, but Shelby had been shot with a 9mm of a specially tailored shell made by the gun maker Stechkin for their mark 5 model. It had taken some time to identify the shell but made easier by the cartridge case found on site.

Vitriano had said his gun was a Luger 32 calibre. That meant that he was lying or he was never at the site. The cartridge case was found at the scene close to some tyre tracks which might indicate that the person firing leant out of the car window. The tyre marks were identified as those made by the tyres on the Range Rover driven by Vitriano. The next thing they had to do was get Vitriano's gun in for inspection and test firing.

Birch picked up the phone 'Mr Vitriano, we're carrying out an inspection of guns in the area in order to rule out individuals. Would you be inconvenienced greatly if I asked you to drop your gun in to the police station when you have time. I understand that you are a Russian national applying for Canadian citizenship?'

'Yes that is correct and I would be happy to bring in my gun.'

'I expect it's a Russian made gun.'

'That is correct.'

'Thank you. Goodbye Sir.'

Vitriano lived in a very quiet road where every house was a large front garden with a spacious drive and a double garage. The result being that apart from the occasional delivery van, there was never any need for anyone to park in the road.

So he was very suspicious when he began seeing a black Buick parked every morning outside the house opposite his. The Buick left after four hours when a grey Ford took over. That was replaced for the next four hours when another car took over.

The routine had become so regular over the last week that he knew the shift patterns. Four cars stood watch for four hours each over a twenty four hour period. He was obviously being watched.

During that week he received a letter informing him that his application for citizenship had been refused. He also received a letter from his brokers telling him that his request to purchase stock in Legat Mining had been turned down.

He fell heavily into the upholstered chair at his desk and held his head in his hands. He'd clearly been black listed. The next step was deportation or prison or both. He was obviously suspected of the shooting up at Bear Lake. If they pulled him in for that he would be locked up for fifteen years and deported afterwards. He struggled with that scenario, it was a real possibility.

Vitriano was subsequently found dead in his study with a bullet in his head.

In an enquiry into the shootings at Great Bear Lake it was decided that Shelby and Legat had shot each other simultaneously and Vitriano had shot Simon probably by accident.

Simon flew out to the property to bring Mac up to date with the latest developments. Initially the meeting was frosty, as if Mac somehow held Simon responsible for Mark's death. It appeared that Mac suspected some kind of subterfuge. Simon realised that Mac had lost a friend in Mark and would be suspicious of everyone for some time.

'Mac,' he decided to cut through the emotional blockage, 'I've decided to accept the directorship of the company, unless you have any objections. As you know the company was about to go under with the loss of capital. I have injected sufficient funds to keep the company afloat until we produce marketable minerals. We must keep the company within the family so to speak now that it's about to show results after all the years of investigation.

I have no plans to interfere with the structure of the company, you will remain general manager with a shareholding. I will take over the position of managing director, being the major shareholder. My main concern will be financial management.'

Mac had a cool head and had a disdain for pontificating. He was happy in his job because he was skilled at it. Life held no difficulties, to him difficulties only existed for people who were incapable of doing their job.

'When will I have money to take on more hands? If I'm to produce the minerals quickly I will need to erect two more rigs' he said.

Simon rubbed his chin and said 'We have to wait for the money to come through before we can spend it Mac. Give me a couple of days and I'll get back to you.'

Simon caught the plane back.

He walked over from the landing apron and headed to the car park. He felt tired. It had been a long day. He drove out of the airport and hit the road to Winnipeg.

He'd only been driving for about twenty minutes through the slushy road when his eyes began to close. He decided to pull in at the first hotel he came to, before he fell asleep at the wheel.

He was driving through Regina, a stone's throw from Saskatoon airport, when he saw the Bull and Thistle Hotel. He pulled in to the car park. It had been a long day and he felt bushed. As he parked he noticed a woman step out of the car in front. Dressed in a fur coat and hat he saw a sparkle of a tiny diamond on each ear, just below the fur hat. As she walked away she displayed a three quarter length coat and knee length suede boots.

Quite pleasant he thought as he stepped out of the car. He made his way to the reception and ordered a room for the night and went into the bar. He sat heavily into a deep buttoned armchair and was immediately joined by a waiter. He ordered a dry Martini, the menu for dinner and an evening paper.

He had no sooner got involved in the paper and his drink when a female voice said 'Do you mind if I sit here?'

'Not at all' he replied and noticed the tiny sparklers just below the line of the fur hat. She had removed the fur coat and was now in a twin set with diamond necklace around her neck. A knee length tweed skirt covered the bottom half. She confirmed his original impression. Quite delightful he thought.

He looked around the bar and then at her and remarked how busy it was.

'Have you eaten here before?' she asked.

'No, have you?' he smiled.

'Yes, but I don't come here very often. I can say without fear of contradiction that the food here is infinitely superior to most restaurants and the menu is incredible. People come here from miles around for the food and it's full every night.'

The menu arrived and the selection it offered was indeed quite amazing. Simon was very impressed. They both ordered the venison and apricots preceded by cauliflower and cheese soup.

They ordered Martinis and Simon said 'You're right about the menu, it's quite amazing.'

She smiled. 'I know' she said. 'I knew you'd be surprised.'

'I should introduce myself. My name is Simon' he said.

She laughed and held out a hand 'I'm Cynthia'.
'Where are you driving to Cynthia?'
'Winnipeg' she replied 'and you?'
'The same' he said.
'I've just come up from Billings Montana. I was there to discuss the sale of five of my horses. I have a trainer down there who's quite a decent chap. I've dealt with him for some years.'
The waiter arrived to say that dinner was served. They finished their drinks and followed him in to the dining room. Simon ordered the house red with the main course and a dry white with the soup which was deliciously creamy. Cynthia said she was glad she chose that soup.
'How many horses have you?' Simon asked.
'Seven. But I'll only have two when I've sold these five.'
'Why are you dispensing with five?' Simon asked.
'My husband died last year and living on my own I don't need the work. I'm keeping two for riding, that's all I need.'
'Are the horses thoroughbred?'
'The two I'm keeping are. Do you ride?'
'No I never had time. How often do you ride?'
'I try to ride every day. Perhaps you'll join me for a riding lesson one day.' She smiled.
They paused as the waiter came to serve the main course, a task carried out in the most theatrical manner designed to command the total attention of all the diners, not just those he was serving, but the whole restaurant. The space around the table was taken up by a flurry of arms and cloths worthy of the most accomplished thespian.
The wine waiter however, who poured a sample of red into a glass and asked Simon to test it, was much more businesslike and less of a showman. The wine was first class as Simon indicated when he asked the waiter to continue pouring in both glasses.
'Are you in business Simon?' Cynthia continued after the display.
'I'm a financial adviser and as of yesterday I am the managing director of Legat Mining' he answered in a disinterested way.
Cynthia complimented him on his choice of wine. He dismissed it with 'They obviously have a good cellar'.
'Do you live alone?' she asked.
Simon replied 'Yes' and then went on to describe his experiences over the recent past. Cynthia listened intently to every detail.

When he'd finished her hand was covering her mouth and he saw that she had tears in her eyes.

'Oh Simon I'm so sorry' she choked.

'So am I' he said looking down at the tablecloth.

They finished the meal in silence. The dinner plates were taken away and cheesecake was served.

Simon cleared his throat and said 'I might take you up on your offer of horse riding lessons'.

'Please do Simon. I'll leave you my number. You must call me as soon as you're free.'

They continued for an hour over coffee and brandy and Cynthia explained that she was a publisher. Simon gave her his copy of THE ILLUSIVE DIAMOND and asked her to read it. She scanned the first page and said she would love to.

They exchanged telephone numbers and parted company around midnight going to their separate rooms. Simon showered and crawled into bed. As he closed his eyes he thought back over the evening and hoped he and Cynthia would meet again.

A week later in her office, she pursed her lips as she looked out of the large window. The sun was strong and bright and the view she had of the open snowscape before her seemed to be one she had never seen before. It was the most beautiful scene she had ever witnessed and she'd been in this office for ten years. Why hadn't she been aware of that view before she asked herself.

She turned and scanned the top of her desk. She was brought back to earth by the two manuscripts awaiting her attention.

She had to proof read them before sending them to the printers today but she just could not stay focused. It was Simon. He was on her mind all the time since their meeting.

She thought about him. She thought about the intensity of his voice and the underlying tenderness of his manner. The aristocratic decadence of his good looks. His extraordinary intellect and his exceptional ability to analyse and reason. He was so sophisticated with such a pleasant personality. Having experienced such injustices as he described to her he was just seeking justice and was not making any great demands on life. Was it possible that she could help him through this period of adjustment in his life. Was it possible that she could share her life with Simon.

She was in her mid forties and was ready to give up business life and settle down. She would ring Simon tonight.

He was drinking coffee in the kitchen when the phone jangled. He took the instrument off the hook on the wall.

'Hello Mr Neufelt' said the voice at the other end. 'Ivan Petrov here of Shirnoff Vodka. I just wanted to advise you of another get together at the Russian Trade Mission next Wednesday. Might I send you an invitation?' Simon paused until he recognised the Russian accent.

'Yes, send me two would you?' he suddenly thought of Cynthia.

'With pleasure Mr Neufelt.'

Simon returned the phone to its cradle and wondered what he did with Cynthia's business card. He went to his jacket hanging on a hook on the wall. He found the card in the pocket and dialled her number.

After six rings she answered 'Hello'. A nice telephone voice, he thought.

'Hello Cynthia.'

'Simon' she squealed.

'Cynthia, I've got some kind of thing for Wednesday evening. Would you like to come?'

'Love to. Is it a business function?'

'No, it's a Vodka presentation at the Russian Embassy.'

'Yes, all right, I'll pick you up, shall I?'

'Good idea.'

'Around seven all right?'

'Perfect.'

Cynthia scanned her bookshelves for the book that Simon had asked her to read. Her gaze fell upon the cover. She slid the book from the shelf and read the title on the dust jacket, THE ILLUSIVE DIAMOND. A warm feeling ran down her spine. She felt as if Simon had stepped into the room.

She flicked through the pages and saw the sketches that Simon had described. She stopped and read the captions under each. The pencil lines came to life. It was as if Mark was standing there beside her explaining the drawings as his pencil moved across the page just as Simon had described.

She browsed through the book flicking the pages, then turned to the synopsis on the back of the dust jacket and read:

This is the story of a man who spent his entire working life mapping the Northern Territories of Canada. With this book the intending prospector could not only find the diamonds but also learn how to dig them up.

Mark Legat is a qualified, highly respected geologist who has spent thirty years in the diamond fields.

She flicked through the pages again and came back to the first page. Sitting down in an easy chair she began to read.

THE ILLUSIVE DIAMOND

Canada is the second largest country in the world. From the arctic north to the huge grasslands of the south this vast country experiences wide extremes of climate. Most of the known minerals are mined including oil, gas and iron ore. Bauxite, copper, nickel, gold and silver are all in abundant quantities and in recent years diamonds have been discovered. In spite of this wealth of resources it remains one of the most under exploited countries in the world.

In northern Saskatchewan the snow covered roads cut through the endless forests of spruce and poplar which screen the drilling rigs operating in their midst. These rigs are thumping and squeaking for twenty four hours a day and the only people who are mindful of their presence are the nomadic Indians who travel between the sparse, nameless, villages with their reindeer herds and give these rigs a wide berth because the reindeer are frightened of the noise.

The rigs are as sparse as the villages and can be hundreds of miles apart. They are used as landmarks by the Indians and can vary from one solitary rig standing alone to dozens in a group.

Since time began this huge land mass has been covered in ice. The varying temperatures have forced the ice sheet to move continually from east to west. As these early ice sheets travelled across the landscape they carried with them minerals from one place to the next. These minerals we now refer to as indicator minerals. They indicate the presence of other minerals deeper in the soil.

In this instance the known indicator is Kimberlite and the mineral it indicates is carbon known as diamonds.

How is the diamond formed? This is the question on everyone's

The Illusive Diamond

lips. I hear you say: If we can learn the formula we can make our own and save the expense and the risk involved in the present production process.

The answer to that eternal question is: It takes a million years for the diamond to reach the condition we describe as a thing of beauty and in the following pages I will attempt to explain the how and the why of the diamond creation and why we have come to regard it as precious.

First, we must go back a million years or so. During this time the earth, as we know it, was still being created. Mountains were being shaped and valleys were being formed. One hundred miles below the surface of the earth where the heat is beyond our comprehension, volcanic explosions took place in various places around the globe and molten rock was forced upwards at astronomical speeds, cooling as it approached the surface.

This phenomenon still occurs today. In the larger dimension we call them volcanoes and stay away from them because the heat they radiate is sufficient to kill us. The smaller edition, considerably older, is the one we are able to deal with and is the one we shall be referring to in this book.

The molten rock travelling upwards cools as it reaches the surface and forms a cone shape. As it cools it takes on the structure of the rock we call Kimberlite.

After two evenings she'd finished reading the book and was impressed. She would like to publish it. She suspected that it was no longer in print, she would have to find out.

The following morning she was able to confirm her suspicions when she spoke to the publisher. Since Simon owned the book he could instruct her to publish it. She would have to speak to her legal department and she would speak to her translator about printing it in foreign languages.

She phoned Simon.

'Simon' the sound of her soft voice took him by surprise.

'Cynthia.'

'I've read the book!'

'Already?'

She laughed 'You forget that reading is my business. I read very fast.'

'Yes I had forgotten. What is your opinion?'

'It certainly has a market but I would say a limited one. It's been around for a few years now. This country is saturated so we must explore foreign markets.'

'Specifically?'

'Well, initially I would think it wants to be countries where it would identify with the national product.'

'The only country I can think of with a similar geography to Canada is Russia.'

'That's true' she said 'and I have spoken to my translator on that point and I can get translations done in Russian but I am limited to one dialect and there are many in Russia. Simon, are you sure you have legal ownership of the book?'

'Yes I'm sure, but if you prefer I'll speak to the company accountants and get their advice.'

'You would be wise to confirm legal ownership if you want to republish. Of course I will do that for you.'

They hung up. Simon considered the conversation. He was surprised at the suggestion that the book could be marketed abroad. Surely the cost involved in translating a technical book offering limited sales would be prohibitive.

Cynthia also considered the conversation but she was kicking around an idea which had broader dimensions. She would enlist one of her authors to add a new dimension to the book. She would see if the scope of the book could be widened to include a love interest. That would widen interest and readership.

CHAPTER 10

'I'm going riding' she said 'would you like to join me?'

It was quite early when Cynthia had decided to ring Simon. His tyres crunched the gravel as he left the drive and joined the freeway. She had given him the address of the stables and the time she would be there so he would have no problem finding it.

He arrived at the entrance and drove under the signboard that spanned the driveway. As he cruised up to the parking lot he spotted her saddling a horse in the paddock. He parked the car and walked over to her. His greeting surprised her. She turned and returned his greeting warmly.

Another female bounced out of the stable door leading a second horse that was already saddled.

'Here's Duke' she called as she approached Cynthia. 'He's all ready to go.'

'Mary, this is Simon. Simon this is Mary.'

'Hi!' Mary happily waved over at Simon.

'Hello' Simon responded.

They mounted their animals and walked sedately out of the paddock. As they rode away Cynthia explained the foibles of each animal and they made their way into a lightly wooded area. She described the handling technique of Simon's horse and questioned him with regard to his experience with horses. Simon explained that he felt quite comfortable even though it was some years since he was on a horse. Cynthia gradually increased the speed to a trot as she described the necessity of a good seat. After an hour she decided it was time to return.

'The clouds tell me that it's going to rain so I would like to get back before it starts.'

Cynthia increased the pace and they arrived back at the stable just as the rain started.

Mary met them at the stable door and ushered them in. As soon as they dismounted she began wiping the animals down and walked them into their respective stalls. They gave them feed and water as the rain increased in intensity.

'How long will this last I wonder?' asked Simon as he searched the horizon from the open door.

'You won't be going anywhere tonight' Mary shouted against the noise of the rain on the roof.

After they finished tending the horses she called 'Follow me'. She led them through a passage that was divided up by three doors and ultimately took them to some living quarters which comprised a complete flat. 'I use this on just such occasions' she said. 'Make yourself comfortable,' she pointed at the two easy chairs as she walked through to the kitchen, 'while I see what we've got to eat'.

Cynthia followed her as Simon dropped into one of the chairs. Cynthia called 'I'd like to take a shower Mary'.

'Help yourself' came the reply as Cynthia disappeared into the bathroom.

After ten minutes Mary came into the living room. 'We have fish with salad' she announced.

'Fantastic!' Simon rubbed his hands together.

'You'll be staying the night of course' she added.

'Of course' Simon accepted.

They agreed to follow each other into the shower and then Mary proved that she could cook fish. Two bottles of Chablis were shown justice as they listened to the rain pelting down, hammering against the doors with the wind gusting against the windows.

'It's clear that you could never have driven home tonight' Mary observed as she looked out of the small window.

'That's true' agreed Cynthia.

After an hour of chatting and laughing Cynthia stood up and said 'I'm very tired Mary, if you don't mind I'll go to bed'. Then she disappeared into the small bedroom.

'Where would you like me?' Simon asked Mary.

'You can take your pick, we're both reasonably acceptable I suspect' Mary laughed.

'I,' Simon tested the overstuffed cushions on the sofa, 'will crash here, if that's all right'.

'If that's acceptable. Otherwise you can have the other bed. The only inconvenience is that I'll be in it.' She laughed again.

'This will do fine, I don't need too much sleep.'

'OK' she said dismissively, closing the door behind her as she left.

He'd been lying in the darkened room on the sofa for some minutes with his eyes closed when he was conscious of someone else in the room. He opened his eyes. The rain had stopped and the moonlight was streaming in through the window. In the light of the moon he saw the female silhouette standing in front of the window looking out into the night. It was Mary, she was naked.

'Are you all right?' he asked.

She nodded and walked silently over and joined him on the sofa.

Johnny Caine was eating breakfast and scanning a magazine at the same time. It was a horse dealer's magazine in which horses were bought and sold. He was going to buy these horses of Cynthia's but he had to have someone to take them off him at a profit. His plan was to take the five she wanted to sell and unload three for the same price as he was paying for five. All her animals were from good stock, he knew that, so he was confident of making money.

Since his wife had run off with a top insurance man she was demanding seventy five per cent of their joint holdings with a threat of reporting him to the tax inspectors on certain deals if he gave her any trouble. The current deal he planned to do in cash so that he would be kept out of the books. He never did trust her and he never trusted any insurance man anyway. They're both a pair of crooks so she'll get as little as possible. It was some years ago when she ran off and he wasn't sorry to see the back of her.

That's when he met Cynthia's husband. He was a decent chap.

Johnny Caine had thought about Cynthia ever since their last meeting. She was a good looking woman, so cheerful and self sufficient. Defiant of all about her. She possessed a wonderful confidence that so many must admire.

He had decided to make the trip over to her today to close the deal on the horses and see if she would consider throwing in her lot with him. They had agreed on a notional sum for the horses in discussions when she came over to him but they would have to cut back on that.

It was on that visit that he was reminded how attractive she was and how pleasant she was when she spoke to him. She clearly found him attractive. He'd never been aware of that before.

By the time she left his office on that day he had decided that he wanted to marry her.

She smiled in his direction as she slid into the Chrysler and slammed the door. That confirmed his suspicion that she fancied him.

He remembered the glimpse of her leg as she smoothed her skirt before shutting the door of her car. She didn't have a bad pair of legs either.

He remembered waving and smiling at the image of his future wife as she crunched her way down the gravel drive.

As she pulled away she smiled inwardly at this shapeless tweed jacket and his baggy trousers, his tight mouth and his low lumbering movements.

He obviously cherished his bachelorhood.

He finished his coffee and began dressing, carefully, for this was to be an important meeting. He looked at his suits and narrowed the choice down to the grey Worcester. A white shirt of course and a blue striped tie. He wanted to look sincere and business like. Finally he put on his brown brogue shoes.

He wanted the horses for a good price but he also knew that Cynthia was looking for a husband and he could do with a wife. Cynthia was ideal and she was rich, very rich. She'd inherited all her husband's wealth when he died last year.

He'd always thought that she fancied him so today he would sound her out.

He'd known Cynthia for years and was aware she knew little about horses. She played at publishing and probably knew as much about that as she did about horses. His own business was bad, it always had been, he wasn't really a businessman and he'd had Cynthia in his sights for some time.

He told her that he expected to be at her place around lunchtime when they spoke on the phone yesterday. So he would take her out for lunch and give her the full treatment. As he went out the door he looked at himself in the mirror. He decided he wasn't too bad for forty, in fact he looked pretty good he told himself. She was forty too and she was pretty lucky to pick up a man like him at her age.

He slid into the car feeling good with himself and he pushed the gear shift into drive confidently. His tyres struggled to bite the grass as he headed for the gravel drive.

Johnny arrived at Cynthia's office building and parked at the rear on the parking lot. He walked into the reception and asked for Cynthia. He was sent into her office.

She walked round to the front of her desk to greet him. Her stance was feminine but defiant. The black sheath form-filling dress accentuated all her best features. Her face framed by her long dark hair and simple gold jewellery radiated confidence and poise. Her eyes were alive and gleaming. They stood there for a moment looking into each other's eyes. Were they about to do battle or simply talk? Disarmed by her simple but striking beauty he didn't know the answer.

'Johnny how are you?' she smiled as they shook hands.

'I'm AOK' he laughed. 'And you?'

'I'm fine' she returned his smile. 'Take a seat' she indicated a seating area over by the wall.

'Before we make ourselves comfortable can we go to lunch?' he asked, feeling as if he'd scored his first point by showing his ability to take control.

'What a good idea' she said and walked over to the door. 'Let's go.'

She took him to a very nice restaurant where she was obviously known and they were given a table instantly. She sat quickly showing her familiarity with the place. She sat directly across from him with her back to the other tables.

He sat slowly and a little apprehensively being quite undone by her somewhat businesslike attitude, for which he was totally unprepared. He glanced round at the other tables to see if anyone was listening.

'Cynthia' he began, 'can I give you a cheque for the horses?'

'Of course you can.'

'My problem is that I can't make the figure that we discussed.'

'How much do you want to give for them?'

'I think we were a bit rash in our original estimate to be honest and I think that twenty per cent less would be a more realistic figure.'

'If you say so, that's all right. To be honest I just want to get rid of them' she said sadly looking down at the cruet in the centre of the table.

The fussy little waiter arrived for their order and they both ordered boeuf bourgignon. The waiter asked Cynthia did she want wine and she answered 'I have work to do this afternoon'.

When the waiter left Johnny spoke, 'Cynthia'.

'Yes John.'

'There is something else I want to talk to you about.'

'Yes.'

'I'm thinking seriously about settling down. It's also possible that you're thinking along the same lines. Is that so?'

'I think about it from time to time but not seriously.'

The meal was served quickly and silently and the waiter crept away.

'Well Cynthia' Johnny cleared his throat. 'Would you consider marrying me?'

She was shocked and surprised. She didn't know whether to laugh or cry. There was a long period of silence.

The silence was broken only by the muffled sounds of cutlery and crockery and murmuring voices that suddenly became audible. Her mind began racing in all directions. She looked down at her plate. Had she given this man the wrong impression at any time? She thought back over their recent meetings of which there were few. She smiled inwardly at the thought of marrying him. The man was a moron.

She spoke gently 'Johnny, I am sincerely complimented by your offer and I thank you for your consideration, but I should tell you that I do have a man friend with whom I am very close.

He choked on his food. That, he wasn't expecting. He had no idea that there was a man in her life. She watched the colour drain from his face.

'I had no idea' he spluttered. Suddenly, the woman had gone down in this opinion. He cleared his throat and stroked his chin. 'How is your meal?' he asked needing no answer just a change of subject.

'I've never tasted anything so heavenly in all my life' she replied softly.

He ran a hand through his hair. He looked down, he looked up. He looked out of the window at the dark shadows thrown between the tall trees by the strong sunlight. His despairing eyes looked back at her hair and the dappled effect on it caused by the sunlight coming through the lace curtains.

His emotions were running riot in his mind and he eyes had become hard and glass-like.

After lunch they parted company and Cynthia went back to her office, picked up the manuscripts and delivered them to the printers as arranged. Then she went home to change for her meeting with Simon. She was looking forward to their meeting and was quite excited. She had never seen the inside of the Russian Embassy and that alone made their meeting special.

She thought about Johnny's behaviour at lunch and became a little annoyed that he should make such an assumption. It was somewhat immature of him.

At home, she laid out the clothes she would consider wearing tonight and stepped into the shower. Having completed that task, she stepped out of the shower and wrapped in a huge white towel returned to the bedroom, her hips undulating languorously. She stood by the bed, hands on hips and inspected the clothes she had laid out on it.

Allowing the towel to fall she picked up the underwear she had chosen and standing before the full length mirror, slipped into it. Liking what she saw she turned to pick up her outer clothes.

She decided on the suit with the three quarter sleeves. It was calf length and would do nicely with the shoes she liked most.

She sat at the dressing table in her underwear brushing her hair looking down at her jewellery case. The decision on the jewellery made, she slipped on the simple gold and diamond necklace and earrings.

She slid into the pale blue skirt and then the matching jacket. Stepping into the high heeled shoes she took one last look in the full length mirror and left the room shining in confidence.

Climbing into the car she pushed the shift into drive and rolled slowly over the gravel not hearing the phone ringing in the sitting room and she wasn't to hear it at all that evening as it was to ring every hour.

She arrived at Simon's on time and he greeted her with 'Hi!' as he jumped in beside her.

They kissed then she said 'Hi!' As she pulled off the driveway she said 'You'll have to direct me Simon'.

They arrived at the Embassy and entered the function room. As they did so they were greeted by an officious Russian in a black bow tie carrying a tray of drinks. Then they were met by the man that Simon knew.

He approached them and extended a hand saying 'Simon how are you?'

Simon turned to face Cynthia and said 'May I introduce Cynthia'.

The Russian extended his hand once more and said 'My name is Ivan

Petrov, I'm pleased to meet you', his face wreathed in the salesman's smile.

'What a lovely room this is' Cynthia said looking up at the huge crystal chandeliers suspended from the ceiling.

'Yes we're very proud of this room' the Russian said with a sweep of his hand.

'The decoration is breathtaking' Simon said looking up.

'The room was designed by a top Russian designer from Moscow. Most of his work is carried out at the palaces in St Petersburg' Ivan said expansively.

They spent the evening mingling and drinking and Cynthia utilised the occasion to publicise her company at which she was expert. During the evening they consumed a reasonable amount of Vodka and eventually ordered four cases of the stuff. Caviar was on hand by the bucketful and they both had their fair share.

At midnight they left and drove back to Simon's place. It started to rain as they joined the traffic and the wipers squealed on the dry screen. As they pulled onto Simon's driveway the rain became much heavier and Simon opened the double garage door with the remote on his key ring. Cynthia was impressed.

They curled up on the sofa, drank coffee and crunched biscuits. Simon said 'I'm thinking of driving to San Francisco, would you like to join me?'

'Yes I would' she looked up at him and smiled.

'I'm staying in the Bay area. I have a friend there.'

'Sounds good' she said, 'when does this happen?'

'Next week' he replied 'about Wednesday'.

They talked for about an hour then Simon said 'I take it you're staying the night?'

'If that's all right with you' she said smiling.

'Of course' he laughed.

'I'll just use the bathroom if I may.'

'Feel free.'

She stood and took clips from her hair and shook her hair violently and stepped out of her shoes. Turning to Simon she said 'Please excuse me for one moment'.

She tip-toed silently across the floor, her hair cascading over her shoulders. As she reached the bathroom door she stopped, turned and smiled at Simon. Then she walked in and closed the door gently behind her.

It occurred to Simon at that moment that she looked positively ravishing. He inhaled and shook his head in disbelief. It was now 2 a.m.

He went into his shower room threw off his clothes and showered. He thought about San Francisco and the friend they were staying with there. He thought they would all enjoy themselves.

He towelled himself down as he walked through into the bedroom. He crawled into bed and buried his head in the pillow. It wasn't long before he drifted into a deep, much needed sleep.

Twenty minutes passed and he was shaken awake by Cynthia as she climbed in beside him.

The following day she left the office promptly. She drove home feeling good with herself and she was looking forward to a drink. She opened the front entrance door and went straight to the bedroom and threw off her day clothes and slipped into her house dress.

She went down to the kitchen and poured a gin and tonic. She filled the kettle with water and went to the refrigerator. Taking out a handful of green salad she placed it on the chopping board and began chopping it up.

After only five minutes she heard the crunch of tyres on the drive. Who the hell can that be, she asked herself aloud. She walked over to the kitchen door and opened it. She recognised the Range Rover.

'Oh no!' she cried. Leaving the door open she returned to the chopping. A step on the quarry tiled floor made her turn towards the door. Johnny had stepped over the threshold.

'Cynthia!' he shouted.

'Johnny!' she returned the greeting.

'I've been trying to reach you' he said in mock concern.

'Why?' she asked as she opened the fridge.

'I want to arrange for the big truck to come over to pick up the horses.'

'Whenever you wish John' she took ham from the fridge.

'I'd like to do it tomorrow.'

'That's OK' she plopped the ham on the plate.

'Are you staying to eat?' she asked hoping he wasn't.

'No thanks, I'm meeting a couple of lads.' She turned and appraised

his appearance. Yes, he had his usual clothes on, baggy cords, shaggy jacket. 'Where have you been? I was phoning you all evening last night.'
'I went to a function.'
'I was ringing 'til two in the morning.'
'Was it that urgent?'
'I was concerned.'
'Johnny, I've been looking after myself for years.'
'Where were you 'til after two in the morning?'
'Johnny, it's not your concern. But if you must know I stayed at a friend's place.'
'Don't tell me … it was your … man friend' he spat out the words. She piled the salad stuff onto the plate with the ham and began slicing the tomato.
'As a matter of fact, yes' she said as she placed the slices of tomato on the plate.
'You tramp!'
She turned round slowly to face him, 'I beg your pardon'.
'You behave this way even though you are aware of my feelings towards you. You're a tramp.'
'What gives you the right to judge me, may I ask?'
'You know my feelings towards you.'
'I thought we clarified that position at lunch two days ago. I shall do as I wish and I think it's time for you to leave, and I mean now!'
He took two short sharp steps towards her, his open hand struck her across the right cheek sending her spinning away from him. Losing her balance she fell to the floor striking her head on the hard stone and was momentarily dazed. She let out a little scream of shock.
They didn't hear the sound of a second set of tyres rolling over the drive as Simon arrived. He heard the scuffling sound, ran to the kitchen door and burst in.
'What the hell is going on?' he shouted as he was confronted by the scene in the kitchen. He was facing Johnny's back who was standing over Cynthia's prostrate body with his hand raised. Johnny spun round to face the intruder.
'Mind your own business' he shouted back. Guessing this was the man responsible for his insane jealousy, the man on whom he could release his pent up rage for stealing the object of his desire.
Simon saw Cynthia holding her red cheek lying on the floor, quickly took stock of the situation as he stared at Johnny's glass-like eyes. No

further dialogue was needed between the two men. Simon took a swing at the other man's face. The only sound was a muffled grunt as Johnny staggered backwards falling into the worktop where Cynthia had dropped the knife.

In a flash Johnny picked up the knife and charged back at Simon. The two men were now locked in a violent struggle, Simon wildly hitting the other man to ward off the wielding dagger. Frantically Johnny was stabbing the air hoping to catch Simon with it. He inflicted six slight cuts as Simon managed to land some worthwhile blows with his fist rendering the other man weaker.

Paralysed in fear, shaking from head to toe, streaming eyes, Cynthia, lying on the floor, had drawn up her legs into the foetal position for fear of the men falling over them and crashing down on top of her. The sight of the two six foot men wrestling in front and above her had assumed the proportions of a spectacular and not something to be dropped from above.

The fresh clean air of her pristine kitchen was now invaded by the smells of perspiration and men's bodies. The grunts and groans of the two men terrified her from her position looking up at them. Her kitchen had now become an arena where the two men were fighting to the death.

Johnny had become a raging bull with eyes bulging; a man demented, swinging and thrusting the knife in every direction.

Simon's face had the look of a man terrified of an opponent charging towards him with a knife, not knowing why he was being attacked or who was doing the attacking.

Cynthia curled on the floor, biting her knuckles, feeling guilty in some mysterious way for being the cause of this bloody contest screamed 'Stop it!' but she had no effect on the struggling men, her voice being muffled by the sounds of the frenzy.

Simon was bleeding in six places on chest and arms and blood was splashing everywhere. Johnny was still frantically stabbing at Simon again and again, while attempting to duck the punches but not always successfully and collected some colourful bruises.

CHAPTER 11

The two men rolled around the periphery of the room in the ongoing struggle. They knocked over furniture and pots and pans in a cacophony of noise along with grunts and groans of men making the superhuman effort.

Having completed a second circuit of the kitchen Johnny managed an upwards thrust with the knife that just perforated Simon's anorak. Before complete penetration occurred Simon caught the man's wrist as the swing was in motion tightening the curve upwards and assisting the thrust. The knife penetrated the man's neck under the chin. Johnny collapsed to the floor, a lifeless heap, emitting a pitiful moan.

Simon fell heavily against the fridge all strength drained from his body. Cynthia had crawled backwards to the wall and had remained frozen with fear in that position throughout the fracas with knees under her chin. Now she crawled from her position to inspect Johnny who was now prostrate on the floor, lifeless. As she bent over him blood welled from his mouth and saturated his clothes. Tears flooded her eyes as she felt his wrist and identified a fading pulse.

Simon staggered over to help her to a chair and they both sat down to regain some strength. Eventually, after a minute or so Simon phoned the police by which time Cynthia was deeply distressed. Apart from Cynthia's muffled sobs the kitchen was now silent.

The police arrived and the man in charge surveyed the scene that confronted him in the kitchen. He took a deep breath through his teeth and looked at the blood covered floor.

He stepped over to the body on the floor and bent down to make a closer inspection. The blood pumping from the mouth had now subsided. He held the wrist to confirm the lack of pulse and looked at the knife still protruding from the neck. He turned to another officer and gave instructions to radio for an ambulance.

A policewoman comforted Cynthia whose nervous state had deteriorated. The chief officer asked if Simon was able to be interviewed and they made their way into another room. Simon's breathing was now slowing down but his heart was still pumping like an oil rig. He was able to tell the story as it had happened and the chief took notes then returned to the kitchen where he sent for a photographer and a doctor.

Sitting down at the table with the police woman and Cynthia he asked if he might interview her now. Between sobs and gasping for air, Cynthia answered 'Yes' and told her story. The policeman asked detailed questions and made notes.

When he was completed the photographer arrived and began taking shots of the scene in general and the body in particular. Then the chief had the body taken away.

The doctor arrived and took a look at Simon's injuries patching him up. Eventually they put Cynthia to bed after the doctor had given her an injection to calm her nerves. Simon found a couch in the sitting room and made himself comfortable on it falling asleep almost immediately.

The ambulance arrived and Simon was carried into it and driven away in minutes. He was asleep for the whole journey and knew nothing of it. He also knew nothing of his arrival at the hospital and his shunting into the reception area, save for a misty vision of white coats and stainless steel as his clothes were removed and he was wheeled into the treatment room where he as given a light anaesthetic.

He was cleaned up with something like antiseptic, the smell of which was to stay with him for days, he was stitched where the wounds were deepest and covered with sticking plaster where they were minor.

He knew nothing of the process since he was unconscious the whole time. When completed he was wheeled into a ward where he remained asleep, occasionally waking for short periods then slipping back into unconsciousness.

Eventually, his eyes opened and his head cleared as he looked around the room. He moved to change his position in the bed and felt the stretching of his skin as the stitches pulled and the sticking plaster refused to move with his flesh.

As he lay there he recalled the happening of three days ago. His muscles tightened and his mouth became dry. He closed his eyes and shook his head in an effort to rid his mind of the picture.

Still in hospital pyjamas, he was finally returned to the house from which he was picked up, Cynthia's house. He was taken into the bedroom and placed into bed by the ambulance men.

The bright sunshine was streaming through the big window when he woke, there were no curtains to defuse the brilliance. It was blinding. He looked around the room to identify his surroundings. He couldn't for the moment remember where he was. He looked down at his pyjamas and recalled his recent past. He heard muffled kitchen sounds and female voices.

He swung his legs over the edge of the bed and pulled himself into a sitting position. Shaking his head he struggled to his feet and pulled on a robe. Heading in the direction of the kitchen sounds he arrived at a pair of swing doors and passing through he found himself in the kitchen.

He saw Cynthia's back, she was standing at the sink. At the sound of the swinging door she spun round and screeched 'Simon!'

With arms outstretched she strode over to him laughing happily and threw her arms around his neck.

'How are you. How do you feel?' she asked leaning back to get a global view.

'OK I guess' he replied meekly.

'Coffee?' she asked.

'Please.'

A voice from the far corner 'Good Morning!'

Simon looked in the direction of the voice as Cynthia called from the coffee pot on the other side of the kitchen 'That's my friend Pam'.

'Good Morning Pam' Simon returned the greeting as Cynthia placed a mug of coffee on the table and pulled out a chair.

'Sit here Simon' she directed.

His mouth was painfully dry and he was glad of the coffee.

'You've both obviously been working extremely hard' he said as he surveyed the room. 'There's no sign of the fracas that happened. You've done a fantastic job.'

'Well we started at nine and it's midday now' Pamela said.

'I must say I had no idea it was so late' he said as he looked at the clock on the wall. He finished his coffee and placed the mug on the table. 'Might I have a bath?' he asked.

'Yes of course' Cynthia answered 'as long as you don't keep Pamela from the shower. She has already asked me if she can take a shower.'

'I promise' he replied.

She took his hand and led him to the bathroom. Once there she helped him remove pyjamas which had partially stuck to the sticking plaster that criss-crossed his chest back and arms. The room was large with marble lined walls and floor. There was a large triangular bath in one corner and a shower cubicle in another.

While the bath filled she helped him out of his clothes and then he stepped in. To his surprise she threw off her clothes and joined him. She carefully sponged between the plaster patches on his arms and chest as she sat facing him in the warm sudsy water.

After a few moments they heard the door close and then the shower door open and close. Cynthia smiled and said 'That's Pamela'. She stood up and asked him to turn round to allow her to do his back.

When she had carefully completed his back she returned to her original position sitting down in front of him to continue washing the front bottom half.

The effect on Simon became immediately obvious and Cynthia looked up at him and smiled. At that moment Pamela stepped out of the shower covered loosely in a robe and walked over to the bath.

'Can you manage?' she asked as she looked at the plaster patches that covered his top half.

'Pam would you dry the top half of his back before the plaster gets wet?' Cynthia asked as she sponged his legs. Pamela dropped the robe, stepped into the bath behind Simon and began dabbing the flesh between the plaster patches with a towel.

Having dried is back she stepped out of the bath, her ample breasts bouncing with a life of their own. She said 'That's done, I'll be off then, you obviously don't want me to do the front' with a smirk.

Cynthia, faced with the obvious result of her loving care, satisfied further pressing needs with oral skills he didn't know she possessed. They completed drying each other off embraced and kiss.

Cynthia said 'There's not many men can boast being in the bath with two females at once'.

'That's true' he replied.

They each threw on a gown and she led him through to a dressing room where she sorted out some clothes of her husband's for Simon to wear whilst she got his clothes washed.

Cynthia went into the kitchen and began preparing something to eat. Simon tried on the various clothes she had sorted out for him and made a choice. He dressed in a shirt and tie pinstriped suit and socks and shoes. He looked in the full length mirror and decided to keep on the outfit and get the girls' opinion.

Slowly he walked along the passage unable to make violent moves for fear of disturbing the plaster and pulling the stitches that would tear his flesh and incur the pain that he had already experienced on more than one occasion.

As he entered the kitchen a scream of delight went up from the women followed by cat calls and whistles.

'That seems to indicate that the clothes are acceptable' he laughed.

'They look lovely. You look clean and wholesome, the way we like you. You look your old self, the clothes could have been made for you.' Cynthia stood with arms outstretched, walked over to him smiling gleefully and kissed him. Standing back, she appraised him and said 'You are the same size as my husband'.

'That's very fortunate' Simon said. They began eating and he said 'I wonder if I could drive?'

'Why?' asked Cynthia.

'I'd like to visit my house' he replied.

'If you feel you must, but I don't think you should drive. Is there anything you're particularly worried about?'

'I have to check my messages.'

'If you must go Simon then I will drive you.'

Simon wanted to stay at home for a few days. He was out of touch living so far from his phone. 'I will stay at home for a day or two and I may need my car.'

'Then I will drive you and Pamela will follow in mine.'

'I don't want to cause you all this trouble.'

'It's no trouble, Pamela and I have to go shopping anyway.'

They finished eating, dressed and climbed into the two cars. The two women dropped Simon off at his house and left him. He went into his house and walked through looking around. It felt cold. In the kitchen he turned up the heating which had turned itself down automatically while he was away. He went to his study sat down at his desk, picked up the phone and took his messages. There was a pile of them. He made notes of the important ones, put the kettle on and took a loaf of bread out of the ice box. Now he felt at home and felt much better.

He spent three days dealing with the various messages on his answering service and generally getting back into the normal routine. Once the house warmed up the place felt more like home again and he felt comfortable.

After a week he remembered that he was to return to the hospital for a check-up and removal of the stitches. As soon as he woke up he went to the window to inspect the weather, something he had missed doing in his absence. Yes the snow was still there.

He dressed and put Cynthia's suit into a bag. He would return that to her on the way to the hospital. He threw his bag in the back of the car and drove away.

Simon unlocked the door and let himself in with the key that Cynthia had given him. He walked through the kitchen where he'd expected to find her and calling her name got no response.

He walked on into the passage and heard breathless giggling and muffled whispering. She was evidently in the bedroom with Pamela. He walked on towards the source of the sound along the carpeted corridor. They were probably in the bedroom trying on clothes or something. He strolled down the passage and as he approached the bedroom door he raised his hand to knock. Finding it ajar he gently pushed it open.

As the door swung open he was presented with the most unbelievable sight.

Frozen in the doorway with hand raised and mouth open he was confronted with the sight of Cynthia and Pamela locked together in a loving embrace, standing by the bed, totally naked and stroking each other with the eagerness of lovers. Clothes were strewn over the floor.

Surprised and shocked he cleared his throat. The two women, equally surprised, froze for one second then gaped in his direction and uttered a strangled 'Oh!' They disengaged and Cynthia released a nervous, dry, laugh. Then the room became engulfed in silence.

Both moved to grab clothes from the floor in slow motion without panic. It was more a deliberate effort to clothe his embarrassment than their own modesty.

They both cried 'Simon' in unison as Cynthia walked hurriedly towards him slipping into a loose dress.

'What a surprise!' she gasped in a dry husky voice, her beautiful face flushed with excitement, as she cast an anxious glance in Pamela's direction. Pamela was disappearing quietly from the room with an armful of clothes.

Simon, speechless from his recent experience, struggled to find words, 'Yes, I do apologise, please forgive me'.

She threw her arms around his neck happily and whispered 'Simon, you have nothing to apologise for. You know you are welcome here at any time day or night. Just walk in, whenever you wish. I'm always pleased to see you.' She kissed him and looked him in the face smiling. 'Let's go in the kitchen and have some coffee' she said.

She thrust her arm through his, turned him round and breezily guided him to the kitchen. In the kitchen she sat him down on a chair at the table as if he was an old man and busied herself with the coffee pot, coffee, eggs and frying pan. Pamela appeared and helped silently. Food was piled on the small breakfast table and they set about the ham and eggs hungrily.

To the muffled sound of cutlery on plates Cynthia said 'So what was your house like Simon?'

'It felt a little strange at first. Snow had piled up against the door and it was quite cold inside. I had to turn on the heating to warm the place up.'

'Were there any messages on your answer phone?' Pamela asked.

'Yes, my answering service had left an enormous amount that I had to deal with. I'm glad I went home.'

He went to the hospital. He was shown into the treatment room where a matronly middle aged nurse removed his shirt then the plasters from his back in a swift businesslike manner followed by the front and arms. Then she gently took out the stitches. She swabbed the wounds to remove the dried blood then swabbed him all over with disinfectant. Finally, she stuck sticking plaster over the larger wounds and left the smaller cuts uncovered to dry naturally telling him to allow as much air as possible to them. Instructing him to return in ten days she bid him goodbye, and he returned to Cynthia's house. On arrival he found Pamela alone.

'Cynthia had to visit the office. She told me to look after you.'

'That was jolly nice of her' Simon said.

'A cup of tea?'

'Please.'

Over tea she asked about the hospital treatment and Simon described it in detail.

'I can smell the disinfectant from her. Can I see what they've done?' she asked.

He pulled off his shirt and she stood up and walked round to his side of the table and inspected his back.

'I think I'll shower to wash away that smell' he said.

She stroked his back gently and helped him with his shirt. 'Yes' she said, 'that smell is rather ghastly'.

He finished his tea as Pam returned to her chair.

'Right!' he said 'I won't be long' and he left the room. Pam washed the two cups looking out of the window thoughtfully.

He went into the bathroom and stripped off. Stepping into the shower cubicle he turned on the water. He poured some liquid soap on his shoulder as the water beat down on him. As he began spreading the soap over his chest he was grasped around the waist by a pair of female arms.

Pamela's voice whispered in his ear 'I think I'll join you if you don't mind'. He raised his arms above his head and turned to face her. She immediately brought her face up close to his and began to lather his back and hips.

'I don't mind at all' he said as water filled his mouth and her large soft breasts pressed against his chest.

The water beat softly down on them as he gently lathered her body. She reached up and slid her arms around his neck kissing him on the mouth, a soapy kiss that heightened the excitement. His hands slid over her body as the suds seeped down over her long legs.

Washing each other was a sensuous joy that Simon had never experienced before and he feared it would be over far too soon for him. They allowed the water to wash off the soap and stepped out of the shower where she cleverly fell to the ground on her back pulling him down on top of her.

Her long legs wrapped around his and locked him in, having her way with him until he collapsed shattered on top of her.

Eventually she stood up and inspected the plasters on his back and said 'I must replace those'. She went to the cabinet and took out some fresh plaster. Tearing off the damp plaster she dabbed his back with a dry towel and replaced the plaster patches with fresh.

The intensity of their encounter surprised Simon but not Pamela who seemed to assume that it was only to be expected. Simon explained that he had to leave to attend to some work. They dressed and chatted in a friendly manner and returned to the kitchen where they found two official looking letters, one addressed to Cynthia, the other addressed to Simon.

Pamela made tea while Simon opened his letter. 'It's from the police with the coroner's report' he said as he scanned the typed pages.

They drank their tea and Simon pushed his letter into his pocket. Walking past her he placed his hand on her shoulder, squeezed gently and left.

Climbing into his car he joined the traffic and headed for home. In his study he dropped into his chair and took out the coroner's letter. The phone on his desk rang. It was Cynthia.

'Simon, you might have waited 'til I got home.'

'I'm sorry my work has piled up here.'

'How is your back?'

'It's a lot better now. It's almost comfortable.'

'I want to see you.'

'Give me twenty four hours and I'll be over.'

'Why don't I come over to you now?'

'Of course, but you have to let me work.'

'If I promise to let you work can I come over?'

'Of course.'

She threw some clothes into a bag and left immediately.

Simon replaced the phone and inhaled deeply through clenched teeth. He returned to the coroner's report and scanned it, then he read it in detail.

THIS IS A POLICE REPORT BASED ON THE CORONER'S VERDICT IN THE MATTER OF THE DEATH OF J CAINE

Mr Caine died as a result of a stab wound to the neck. The wound was inflicted with a 3" bladed knife which passed upwards and penetrated the floor of the mouth. The blow severed the carotid artery and the oesophagus resulting in the stomach filling with blood. The wound is not common in murder victims but may be expected in a deflected blow as described by Mr Neufelt. The wound was inflicted during a struggle when Mr Caine attacked Mr Neufelt for no apparent reason. Mr Neufelt was an innocent bystander who went

> to the aid of a woman who was being beaten by Mr Caine. In his heroic defence of this woman he suffered the following wounds of his own: four 3" long cuts to the back requiring 21 stitches and minor cuts and scratches to the arms and chest. It is therefore concluded that Mr Caine died in the execution of a crime.

Having read it through he paused momentarily and pondered the contents finally placing the letter in the desk drawer.

He made a note on his memo pad to raise a point from the letter when the police returned, which they undoubtedly would.

He flicked through his desk diary to remind himself what he had to deal with and then he heard the crunch of gravel on his drive. Heaving himself out of the chair he walked through to the kitchen and looked out of the window. Recognising Cynthia's car he unlocked the door and opened it as she arrived at the opening.

'How are you?' she asked as they embraced.

He turned and answered 'I must say my back is a lot better without the stitches'.

They walked in, arms around each other and he sat her down at the table.

'Tea?' he asked.

'Please' she replied.

He put the kettle on and walked over to the door and locked it.

'Have you read the police report on the coroner's verdict?' she asked looking down at the table.

'Yes just' he replied as he came back to the table.

She smiled at him as he sat down. She put her arms around his neck and said 'That proves that you're my hero'.

'You don't take sugar in your tea, do you?' He stood up to walk over to the boiling kettle. He made the tea and brought them both a cup over to the table. As he sat down he said 'We must see what needs replacing in your kitchen'.

CHAPTER 12

The next morning over breakfast Simon asked 'What was the connection between you and Johnny Caine?'
Cynthia explained everything in detail.
'So he expected you to marry him for no reason other than he thought he had the right.'
'That's correct, I hardly knew him.'
'Why don't we claim damages for your kitchen and my injuries?'
'I just want to forget him and the whole affair.'
'I understand' Simon said as he placed his hand on hers.
'Have we given up the idea of a visit to San Francisco?' Cynthia asked in order to change the subject.
'Not at all.'
'OK let's plan the day. When would suit you?'
'The day after my next visit to the hospital.'
'When is that?'
'In ten days' time.'
'That sounds reasonable. In fact I'm ready now' she laughed.
'OK I'll arrange it for that day' Simon said.
'Right, I have to go to the office now' she said as she stood and kissed him.
'I'll check the flights to San Francisco' he said as they embraced.
'I'll ring you later today' she said as she went out of the door.
He sat and finished his tea then phoned the airport.

The days flew by and the date they were to leave for San Francisco was closing in. The evening before they were to leave, during dinner, Simon asked Cynthia 'What did your husband do?'

'He was an architect.'

'How did he die?'

'He was shot.'

'Did you find out who was responsible?'

'Yes, a drunken Indian.'

'What were the circumstances?'

'He was on business in Front Street Potters Bar, interviewing a woman about the construction of a house. When he didn't come home for dinner I began to worry. I finally phoned the police at midnight. Almost immediately they phoned me back saying that they had found a body in Front Street which had been taken to the morgue. Would I like to identify it.

'When the police interviewed the local residents, a woman had said that she had been talking to her architect in her kitchen when someone had tried to force the door. When she had unlocked the door a man had run off. Her architect gave chase but didn't return.

'Thirty minutes later she identified the architect lying in the snow with a bullet in his head when the police arrived.

'Her architect was my husband.'

'Was the Indian caught?'

'No but a witness described him and he was apparently known to the police. He was shot later during a burglary in the same road.'

Simon was deep in thought for a moment then said 'Cynthia, I believe your husband was shot outside my house and I know the man that shot him. It was a drunken Indian. He had attacked my friend outside my house and it was my friend who later shot him when he found the Indian had broken into his house and was going through his desk. My friend, Mark, recognised him as a known burglar and a well known no-good character. The Indian pulled a gun but Mark was quicker.

'I didn't see the woman that you mentioned but I did see your husband lying in the snow.'

'Isn't that ironic.'

'Isn't it. What sort of man was he?'

'He was a good man. On the board of three companies and he lectured at a number of colleges. He was also in great demand as an after-dinner speaker. It was my husband who knew Johnny Caine. It was he from whom my husband bought the horses, personally I hardly knew him.

'The woman for whom my husband was working and whose home he was in on the fateful evening, was Pamela.'

'Another irony you will probably be surprised to know is that Mark who shot the Indian was the author of THE ILLUSIVE DIAMOND' Simon said.

'Well I never' Cynthia's hand covered her mouth in surprise.

They landed at San Francisco airport and were met by Simon's friend Errol who greeted them warmly as Simon introduced Errol and Cynthia. Errol then took them back to his house on the hill. He made them tea and they sat and chatted, about how Simon and Cynthia met and generally catching up with Simon's recent past, as Errol cast an approving eye over Cynthia.

Errol turned to Cynthia and said 'I welcome you to the city that boasts the biggest population of homosexuals in the country.'

'Really?' she laughed.

'Oh yes it's quite true. They're not the airy fairy type. They are very macho. They are big strong men. Their most popular mode of dress incorporates black and leather with chains round their waist and neck. They're very sadistic and are responsible for most of the torture and murder cases in the area.'

'Gosh!' Cynthia's hand went to her mouth.

'Anyway, what do you do Cynthia?'

'I'm in publishing. What do you do Errol?'

'I'm an illustrator of children's books.'

'How wonderful.'

Errol took them into his studio and they inspected his work. They completed the evening eating and discussing art, literature and publishing. Errol told them that he had hired a boat and crew to tour the bay the following day. Simon and Cynthia were both excited about that plan. Errol's girlfriend arrived and they finished the evening drinking.

The next day they went down to the bay and picked up the boat that Errol had arranged for them. They pulled out from the shore and joined the other small boats heading out to the sea. It was a perfect morning, ideal for a day on the ocean.

They spent the day fishing in the open sea and the captain pointed out the blue whale and explained that it was the largest living thing on the planet. They spent time sunbathing on the top deck. They ate a picnic on the rear deck and snoozed in the afternoon. It was late afternoon when the captain decided it was time to return so they pulled in the rods, tidied up the decks and started back.

As the Golden Gate came within sight a huge yacht came into view. One hundred feet of pink hull with white superstructure all lit up, her lights sparkling in the water. The surrounding sea was packed with small yachts and pleasure craft moored around her.

The captain pulled in amongst the gathering crowd and anchored. They were suddenly aware of the sound of a piano playing on the deck of the big yacht accompanied by the voice of man and singing a tune that they had all heard on the radio.

The whole area became silent, transfixed by the sound of the beautiful voice. The captain poured drinks on the rear deck and explained that the private party on the big yacht was a secret that everyone who owned a boat knew about and guests to the area were lucky that they chose today to be here because it only happened twice a year.

They spent the whole evening eating and drinking, laughing and chatting under a starry sky made for just such an evening, listening to smoky piano music and the voice of Larry Haywood a singer of stage and radio.

The captain, a man around thirty, amused them with tales of his travels and interests. He was a skier in the winter and in the spring he spent time prospecting for gold in northern California. He was an avid reader and listed the books he'd read.

Cynthia produced THE ILLUSIVE DIAMOND which he scanned and showed an immediate interest in. He asked if he might read it overnight and he would return it in the morning.

Simon enthralled them with his description of the merits of the book and the author. He described Mark's fifteen years spent in the arctic waste known as the North West Territories during his time mapping the area.

He described his own encounter with the mad Indian and with the Eskimos and his travel through the endless miles of forests by sleigh.

He enjoyed reliving those memories in the telling as it brought the whole experience back to life.

Everyone enjoyed themselves and the two girls were struggling to stay awake as the hours passed. The mood was so relaxing as the captain went below to organise a midnight snack. They just sat there and soaked up the atmosphere.

The piano playing got lazier and lazier and the sound of the slopping of the sea against the hull became more pronounced.

The boat sat in the clear water in silence, save for the sounds of the piano and the singer drifting over the water and the slapping of the gentle swell against the hulls crowded beneath the yacht towering above them. The whole scene was lit up in the warm evening sunset.

Errol's boat had a crew of three, a captain, a cabin boy and chef. At the moment they were all busy in the galley preparing the evening meal, the captain preparing drinks.

The two couples were sitting around on the rear deck drinking and listening in a setting that could not have been improved on if it had been designed that way.

Suddenly there was a shout from the galley then a minor explosion followed by a roar of flames then the whole boat was engulfed in a ball of fire that shot up the galley staircase.

The two couples were thrown over the side into the sea in which petroleum was spilling and flames were creeping.

Adjacent boats moved quickly away, grabbing the arms of those people nearest to them reaching up from the sea. Flames now creeping over the sea in increasing speed.

Fire extinguishers appeared over the side of the big yacht and were turned on, showering the sea below as the vessel got under way and the smaller craft put distance between each other.

Simon, Errol and his girlfriend were rescued by separate craft but Cynthia was last to hit the water and the fireball had sucked all the oxygen from the area on the deck where she had been and her lungs had been emptied at the same time. She was unconscious when she hit the water but she was not burnt as she went under.

Cynthia was dragged out of the sea by two men on a small boat. She lay on the deck on her back, unconscious, a strong smell of petrol pervading the air around her. After some thought and debate the two men decided that her clothes would have to come off to remove the possibility of petrol damaging her skin.

Within two seconds she was lying naked on the deck with the two men standing looking down at the body that men have been known to die for. As she lay on her back her generous breasts were dancing to the rhythm of the engine and the two men could not leave the spot on the deck to which they had become attached, standing one each side of the superb body.

One of the men spoke. 'Jeremy, you'd better check our direction before we run into something.'

'OK Nigel.'

Jeremy shook himself and moved sharply towards the wheelhouse. After reading the compass, he spun round and came back to Nigel. 'We've come out to the middle of the ocean!' he screamed.

'How much juice in the tank?' asked Nigel eyes still glued to the body on the floor.

'Enough to take us back Nigel.'

'Right. Get back to the wheel' Nigel shouted as he unbuckled his belt.

Jeremy returned to the wheelhouse and watched Nigel in the mirror having his way with unconscious Cynthia. Task completed he returned to Jeremy at the wheel. 'She stinks of petrol, we've got to wash her down.'

'Can I do that?'

Nigel took the wheel and turned to Jeremy, 'Yes' he said 'you can wash her down. But use warm water and some fresh soap'.

Jeremy went below and got the soap and the bucket of warm water. Returning to the deck he began the washing process on the front of the still unconscious Cynthia.

Nigel watched from the wheelhouse mirror as Jeremy, having completed the washing of the front stood back and viewed his work. Admiring what he saw he immediately threw off his clothes and mounted the body. Nigel shook his head and smiled.

Jeremy, having satisfied himself dressed and joined Nigel at the wheel.

'Was that nice?' Nigel asked.

'Yes thank you Nig.'

Good, take the wheel. You know Jeremy, I think we'll stay out here for a couple of days and have some fun. What do you think of that?'

'I think that's a fantastic idea.' Nigel went out on deck and unbuckled his belt again.

Back at the scene of the fire, the fireboat had arrived and put the fire out.

Errol had identified the bodies of the crew although terribly burnt and dead.

Witnesses to the scene could not account for the missing female and it was presumed she'd drowned. Names and addresses were taken by the police on all boats and police divers were called in to search the sea bed as far as it was possible as depth was known to limit extensive searching.

Jeremy and Nigel were just passing the spot when the fire started and they grabbed Cynthia from the water without stopping. Physically big men they were mountain people and very strong. Hillbillies. Neither could read nor write. They could never be bothered with book larnin' and all that stuff.

Neither knew their parents and they were both bisexual. They'd had their fair share of bar room brawls and had the scars to prove it. They met in a mining camp when they were both in their twenties and had been together ever since. That was twenty years ago. They both felt that they owed loyalty to no-one and they'd never paid tax or social security and the federal government didn't know they existed.

They had lived in a boat for twenty years, occasionally sheltering in a cave which they had made habitable over the years. It was in a cove up by Bodega Head, sheltered from the rough weather, they could pull the boat up on the rocks and carry out maintenance there.

They were both expert shots and lived on game they shot during their expeditions inland. They ate the fish they caught and knew where to get the best crab and oysters which they sold to the shore-side shops and restaurants.

It was three in the morning and the strong moonlight glow bathed the surface of the sea a milky white. Jeremy had turned off the engine and the two sat out on the deck on two crates looking down at Cynthia considering what was to be done with her.

The friends stayed on the police boat assisting in the search. When the police had completed interviewing everyone in the area they allowed everyone to leave.

Orange streaks appeared across the blue grey slate of the sky as dawn broke and the divers admitted defeat in their search for a body. Simon was distraught. Errol took him back to his place.

Over the next twenty four hours Jeremy and Nigel continued to use Cynthia's body as they wished. When she was on deck and the sea breeze lost its searing heat her body cooled dramatically and they took her into the cabin and laid her on a bunk. They each sat beside her in silence, deep in thought.

After a period Nigel wondered 'Is she alive?'

'If she was dead she'd be as stiff as a board' replied Jeremy.

'She's not stiff so she must be alive' observed Nigel.

'She wants warming up so I'll lay beside her' Jeremy said, throwing off his clothes and climbing on to the bunk.

'That's a good idea and I'll lay the other side.' Nigel followed suit.

Each achieving penetration from their chosen position they reached satisfaction and her body temperature did indeed increase. Suddenly she began throwing up with a strong aroma of petrol escaping her lungs. Nigel caught the lot and moved quickly away out to the deck where he washed down in the bucket they kept there for the purpose.

Cynthia came to life and turned to face Jeremy as she scanned her surroundings.

Slowly regaining her vision she gradually focused on his face. She saw a week's growth of beard and a generally revolting individual. She grimaced. She looked around her. She saw a bundle or rags, three chunks of rock, a collection of fishing rods and two rifles on hooks on the wall. The place was a rubbish tip and smelt like a cow shed. But there was a strong smell of the sea.

Nigel came down the three steps from the deck into the cabin. He stopped in his tracks when he saw Cynthia's eyes wide open. He was stark naked and after a double take he grabbed his clothes from the floor and stepped into them.

Cynthia spoke drowsily, 'What is this, where am I?' She removed Jeremy's large hand from her left breast and struggled to sit up pulling a blanket from the floor to cover her breasts.

'You're living with us on our boat' Nigel explained gently. She was suddenly aware of the muffled thumping of seawater against the wooden hull. Nigel said 'I'll make you some tea' and busied himself around the Calor gas stove.

Jeremy jumped up and ran out onto the deck without a word. He began washing himself in the bucket.

Cynthia was suddenly aware that she had been sick and said to Nigel 'I want a wash'.

'I'll organise it for you right away' he said and went to the doorway shouting up to the deck, 'she wants a wash Jeremy'.

'OK, leave it to me' Jeremy answered and filled the bucket with fresh seawater.

Cynthia steadily pulled herself to her feet. Holding on the side of the bunk she stood and looked around getting her bearings.

'Where do I wash?' she asked.

'Up on deck dear' Nigel smiled sweetly looking up from his tea making.

Gripping the unclean blanket tightly round her with one hand she held the handrail with the other as she made her way slowly up the steps to the doorway leading to the deck. Out in the sunshine she was faced with Jeremy still naked.

'Where do I wash?' she asked him.

'There' he pointed to the bucket which he had now placed on a wooden box with a bar of soap and a filthy looking towel.

'GOD!' she screamed. She looked around the deck and out to sea. There was no land in sight.

It was evening and still hot and there was no breeze. She noticed a rope ladder hanging down the side of the boat.

She turned to Jeremy and said 'You'll be going of course. I'm not washing in front of you.'

'Yup. I'm goin down in the cabin.' He immediately went.

No other boats were to be seen. This pile didn't even have a radio. Her mind began to orientate.

She dropped the blanket and climbed down the ladder. Her swimming ability was limited but she could at least get wet and rinse her body. Holding onto the ladder she dropped below the water line and then pulled herself up again returning to the deck. She scrubbed herself down with her hands keeping out of sight of the door.

She turned and looked at the revolting looking towel draped over the box and decided to ignore it. She walked round the side of the cabin to the other end of the deck, trying to marshal her thoughts. What the heck was she doing here?

The warm evening air dried her body as she looked out over the still ocean as far as the horizon and there wasn't a boat to be seen. The sky was the colour of an orange.

She looked around the deck and saw some washing hanging on a line strung across the deck. Were they her clothes? She stepped purposefully over to the line pulled the clothes off the line. Sure enough they were hers. She slipped into them.

Immediately she felt civilised. She turned to go down to the cabin but at the doorway she met Nigel coming out with a cup of tea in his hand.

'I thought you might like a cup of tea' he said. She took the cup from him.

'Thank you.' She studied him for a moment and said 'What shall I call you?'

'Nigel. That's my name. Nigel. What's yours?'

'Cynthia. Nigel can you explain why I had no clothes on?'

'Yes Cynthia. When we dragged you out of the sea you stunk of petrol and I was afraid that it might burn your skin so we took them off you and I washed them for you. Has the smell gone? I do hope they're all right' he said effecting a sickly smile as he stroked the back of her T shirt.

She pulled away, her mouth turned down. He was such a subservient creep. It's no good talking to this one it's the other one who's in charge she guessed.

'Where was it that you dragged me out of the sea?' She sampled the tea.

'Miles from here. You were on a boat that exploded and you were blown out into the sea where we were and we were able to drag you out. As you landed in the sea the water burst into flames it was amazing you didn't burn. It was lucky that we were passing otherwise you would have died that's for sure.

'Jeremy and me, we looked after you. You were unconscious for two days.'

Now she remembered. She was with Simon and his friends on a boat. But that's all she remembered.

'Did you bathe in the sea?' Nigel asked.

'Yes.'

'We don't go into the sea because of the sharks.'

'Sharks? Oh my God!' she screamed.

'Yes dear that's why we wash in the bucket.' He smiled sweetly. She looked down at the harmless looking sea and a shiver ran through her. She drank her tea.

'How is your tea?' Nigel asked.

'Very nice.' She was genuinely surprised how nice it was.

'Good' he said and disappeared down the stairs.

She followed him. At the bottom of the stairs she came face to face with Jeremy. He was fully dressed and he'd obviously been listening to their conversation.

'You were listening to the singer Larry Haywood showing off on his big showy boat' he said looking her straight in the eyes.

'You'll be taking me home soon I expect.' She returned Jeremy's stare.

'You'll be wanting to pay for your passage I expect.' He looked down at her with folded arms.

'What do you fancy to eat tonight?' Nigel called with his face stuck in the battered refrigerator.

'Steak' Jeremy shouted as he turned round to face Nigel's direction. 'In a sandwich.'

'Cynthia, a green salad for you?' Nigel continued.

'Thank you' she called back. She returned to the deck followed in seconds by Nigel.

He pulled out a big tea chest and threw a cloth over it saying 'We'll eat out here tonight shall we?'

'That'll be nice.' She tried to be sociable. He went back downstairs.

After a further ten days Cynthia had collected one black eye, a bruised cheek and a split lip. Urgently looking for a way off the tub she was searching the horizon all day and was seriously frightened of Jeremy. A shadow of her former self she was refusing to eat their food and in that short time had lost weight.

She felt that being in such demented company she was loosing her mind and she wanted to scream all the time.

It was hot on deck and she was hanging out some washing. Jeremy had designed a torture bench on the forward hatch to which she would be strapped and forced to endure the most horrific demands.

Jeremy walked up behind her. 'What are you doing with my shirt on?' he shouted and grabbed the shirt at the back of the neck and ripped it off her leaving her naked to the waist. She turned with her arms crossed in front of her.

'I thought the shirt was Nigel's. I was washing mine and I just wanted something to wear.'

'Leave my clothes alone.'

The crash of the back of his hand spun her backwards and she fell over the hatch cover. She squealed and whimpered holding the side of her face. She lay on her back stretched over the wooden cover, dreading the next episode, her eyes wide with fear.

He grabbed her skirt and pulled if off then rolled her over on to her front. From the corner of her eye she saw him quickly unbuckle his belt. She screamed as the first slash of the belt cut across her back. She rolled over, holding her arms up to protect her face.

'No!' she cried as the strap cut across her arms and the pointed brass end of the strap formed a wheal at the side of her chest cutting the flesh. She screamed again and cried out 'Please Jeremy'.

Nigel appeared. Jeremy shouted 'Strap her down' and they both set about strapping her arms and legs to the hatch cover, sharing jokes and proposals as she cried like a baby.

That completed, the two men spent the rest of the day raping her in turns and throwing buckets of water over her in great bursts of laughter. Finally releasing the straps and walking away leaving her alone and lifeless to struggle inside out of the sun.

The following morning she received the usual punch and a slap from them as she stepped from her bunk and they had shouted the usual insulting remarks as she made her way out to the deck to wash. She washed in the bucket in the warm morning sun and took the clothes from the line that she had washed yesterday and slipped them on and came back in the cabin to make the tea. She filled the kettle as they both made remarks about her clean clothes.

Then Jeremy said 'We need to make a rota to decide who you sleep with each night'.

Nigel said 'I say that we should each have alternate nights so that there's no disagreements'.

Suddenly Cynthia spoke. 'It makes no difference what arrangements you make Nigel because Jeremy will do what he wants. He doesn't care about you or anyone else.'

The kettle came to the boil as Jeremy grabbed her arm and spun her round and she was ready for that regular move of his. As she turned round she smashed the boiling kettle in his face. He ran screaming out on the deck holding his face.

Nigel was speechless and didn't move from his bunk.

'Nigel!' Cynthia screamed. 'Go and start the engine.' She filled the kettle with fresh drinking water from the refrigerator and placed it on the stove as Nigel rushed out to the wheelhouse.

Cynthia walked over to the rifles hanging on the wall and took one down. Opening the bolt she saw it was loaded. Taking the second one down she found that was loaded too. Moving out on deck she pointed a rifle at Jeremy and pulled the trigger.

Jeremy was bending over the bucket when the shot hit him. He fell sideways with the bullet in the buttock. Cynthia, elated with her success pulled the trigger again and the second bullet hit him in the shoulder.

Nigel reached the wheelhouse and had started the engine when he heard the shot. He looked out of the window and thought for a moment. What am I doing, he said to himself.

He returned to the deck where he passed behind Cynthia in his bare feet and went down into the cabin. Reaching the second rifle down from the hook he ran up to the deck.

At the doorway he shouted 'Cynthia!' and pulled the trigger. Her hands went to her stomach and she dropped the rifle as the first shot struck and she was thrown backwards. The second hit her in the chest and she fell dead.

He moved over to Jeremy lying on the deck and bent over him. 'Jeremy are you still with me?'

Jeremy slowly opened his eyes. 'Of course I am you idiot. Get these bullets out of me.'

He stepped over to Cynthia and felt her neck for a pulse there was none. He shouted 'She's dead'.

Taking the two rifles back to the cabin he returned them both to the hooks on the wall. He took a sharp pointed knife from the drawer and a bottle of Scotch from the cupboard.

He poured some Scotch over the wounds in Jeremy and gave him the rest to drink. Then he brought one of the rocks up from the cabin and cut ten foot from a ball of nylon string.

Then he returned to his shipmate lying on the deck.

'Hold on, let's take a look at the damage' he said.

'Shut up and get on with it.' Jeremy was already in pain and took another swig of Scotch.

Nigel inspected the entry points of the bullets which were clean with no blood stains then rolled Jeremy's great body over and found the exit points that were very bloody and messy.

'The slugs have come out the other side and I've got no digging to do. Lie still while I get the First Aid box.' He ran downstairs and in two minutes returned with the box. The contents were scarcely more than folk remedies and placebos.

He covered the wounds and helped Jeremy to his feet and down to his bunk in the cabin.

Back on deck he tied one end of the nylon string round Cynthia's waist and the other end round the rock. Then he pushed her under the handrail and over the side and watched her dragged down and disappear below the surface.

Then he scrubbed the deck with the water from the bucket to remove all the bloodstains. Returning to the wheelhouse he turned the boat round and headed for Bodega Head and the cave.

Simon and Errol were picked up from the sea by separate boats in a comatose condition. The girlfriend was found to be dead on arrival at hospital. The three crewmen were found dead in the sea and badly burnt. All were sent to hospital where Simon and Errol met up again. After returning home Simon was at his wits end. He spent every day trying to find Cynthia. He phoned the police, the customs, the coast guard, in fact he phoned every agency that might have any news of her. He was distraught with worry.

Every other day he and Errol hired a boat to search the area for any visible signs of her. The area was recognisable for miles by the flotsam and jetsam floating on the surface in the immediate area. They were surprised by the number of boats that had been damaged in the accident. The scene resembled a war zone in size and devastation. The police had marked the area with a ring of marker buoys tied together with coloured tape.

One small badly burnt yacht was listing heavily on its mooring, another was upright with half its hull gone, water washing over its deck. Another was identifiable only by the metal mainmast pointing helplessly upwards with its rigging slapping noisily against it resembling the sound of a ghostly bell echoing across the deserted ocean.

As they searched the ghastly scene of devastation they were conscious of a whole range of emotions to which they were unaccustomed especially when they met the relatives of their crew members who were salvaging recognisable items. Errol reached down and scooped a book floating in the water. It was THE ILLUSIVE DIAMOND.

Leaning on the gunnel he held the book over the water to drain and watched it release the unbelievable amount of water that it had absorbed in its fabric. He stood up and allowed the remaining water to drain. He gave it to Simon. Simon recognised the book at once.

'Hold on to that' he said handing it back to Errol giving no indication that he was aware of the significance of the find. His mind was so full of grief he was unable to comprehend the significance of anything at all other than the matter in hand.

His eyes returned to the search area which he regarded as a cemetery. All was silent except for the slapping of the gentle swell on the side of the boat and somewhere out there a buoy was clanging as it rode the tide warning passing traffic to stay clear of the area and watch out for obstacles below the water line. The hollow sound seemed to come from outer space. It was eerie and seemed strangely fitting.

The relatives of the crew members eventually ended their search and left the area. Simon and Errol decided to end their rummaging through the surface of the sea and leave.

They let themselves into the apartment with a sigh of weariness and collapsed in chairs exhausted. It had been a long day but a worthwhile day. After a long period of silence they decided that they had to get down to the disheartening chore of searching out and questioning agencies or witnesses.

The two men shared the following weeks of mutual misery living on a knife edge, waiting for news. They discussed the numerous ways in which Cynthia may have disappeared. The possibility that the tide may have taken her body and the various routes that might have taken.

Eventually, Simon decided to return to Canada, after extracting a promise from Errol to contact him should anything develop.

The flight back began with him deep in thought and finished with him in deep sleep. On arrival at this house he found the cold something of a shock. As he walked slowly across the gravel of the drive, fighting the biting wind the bitter cold cut into his face. It was so long since he had left home to visit the warm sunshine of San Francisco he'd forgotten how cold it could be in Winnipeg. His unmarked face now lined, showed the signs of the strain of the last month or so and was no match for the cutting edge of the wind.

Physically and mentally exhausted, lacking solid sleep for the last few weeks and weakened by despair, he wanted nothing more than to fall into unconsciousness. He was suffering from a deep depression and carrying a heavy guilt and remorse.

It seemed that everyone around him was dying and he felt totally responsible. First it was Sarah then Mark now Cynthia and the crew of the yacht. He entered the kitchen, slammed the door behind him and dropped heavily into a chair, crashing his elbows onto the table.

He looked up at the ceiling and cried out to nobody in particular 'GOD how much longer must it go on'.

He'd been home a whole week when he remembered that he hadn't told Pamela the bad news. After a week of little eating and total misery he was very weak and this was not a task that he wanted. However, he finally faced up to it and dialled her number.

When she heard the news she collapsed into hysterics and couldn't stop sobbing. After what seemed ages he finally had to break off and hang up. After two days she phoned back and invited him to join her at her favourite restaurant. It took some time to persuade him but he eventually accepted.

They met at the arranged place and when she saw him she was shocked. His face was now very drawn and his eyes were sunken surrounded by dark rings. She couldn't believe the change in him. They embraced and she guided him into the restaurant and a table where they sat and she spent the first five minutes studying his haggard face.

Over the meal she gently drew him on every detail of the accident. The conversation was understandably all about Cynthia and of course the accident. Pamela was in tears all the time and Simon was not happy reliving the affair but she kept firing questions at him albeit in a most gentle manner.

Neither of them ate very much and Simon was glad when the evening ended. She was a nice girl but he wasn't in the mood for her tonight.

They parted with Pam promising to call him within twenty four hours and Simon's shirt stained in her tears.

Simon answered the knock on the door. It was Pamela.

'Hello Pam. Come in . Coffee?'

'Please.'

'How are you Pam?'

'I'm OK. But the reason I came to see you is to see how you're holding up.'

'Well the answer to that is that I'm not very good company at the moment and I don't know if I'm holding up.'

'I know what you mean Simon. I feel the same but at moments like this we should pool our grief.'

He poured the coffee and gave her a cup. 'You don't understand Pam. I am totally responsible for what happened to her.'

Cynthia had told Simon that Pam was a psychologist and he wasn't in the mood to listen to one of her lectures.

'Simon, that's quite a normal reaction.'

'It's not a reaction it's a fact.'

'I see, you caused the explosion.'

Simon looked her straight in the eyes, his lips taut and turning he walked to the other side of the room.

She followed him. 'Simon let's sit down and drink our coffee.'

He pulled out two chairs and they both sat down at the table with their coffee.

Her hand stroked the side of his face. 'Simon just talk about it. I will listen.'

He looked away and focused on a wall at the other side of the room.

'Simon, my darling, we have to learn to live with our losses. Tell me the first thing that comes into your mind and just talk. I will listen I promise. It doesn't have to form any pattern or make any sense. Just garble away and I'll make sense of it if I need to. But I don't necessarily have to make sense of anything. It's just an exercise in clearing the mind.

'There is no time limit. Just start when you feel like it when and where you wish and finish when and where you wish. I'm here as long as you want me I have no other plans I'm all yours.'

They embraced and she kissed him passionately. Then she repeated 'I'm all yours darling'.

'I have no problem with that Pam.'

They sat in silence for some time then Simon said 'The main thing that troubles me is that I don't know where she's lying. I don't really know if she is actually dead. She may be in Jamaica by now. Washed out by the tide.'

Now he had tears in his eyes. She bent over and kissed him. Now she had tears in her eyes. They caressed.

'At times like this it is essential that we maintain a connection with the outside world, friends, neighbours and other people in general, in that way we keep a perspective.

'In the first place I should explain that I have always received good vibrations from you so there is no possibility that I could hold you responsible for Cynthia's death. You and Cynthia are both good people.'

'Are there people from whom you get bad vibrations?' Simon asked facetiously.

'Oh yes. Not everyone picks up vibes. Animals pick them up better than humans and vibrations can come from articles not just people. A cat or dog will never stay in a house where they get bad vibes.'

Simon got up and walked over to the door when the post dropped through the letter box. He picked up a small parcel and returned to the table tearing open the wrapping paper. THE ILLUSIVE DIAMOND was revealed and a letter. He scanned the letter and explained. 'It's a letter from Errol in San Francisco. He says that he is returning the book that Cynthia left. He hopes I am well.'

'Now that book gives off bad vibes Simon.'

'It does? How can a book give off bad vibes?'

'I don't know how, but that book does Simon.'

'Can you feel vibrations now?'

'Yes. I've hated the book since I first set eyes on it years ago when my father first brought it home.'

'Your father brought it home years ago? Was he reading it then?'

'My father was co-author of it.'

'Who was your father?'

'Dennis Shelby.'

'Good gracious!'

'Why do you say that?'

'Because I understood that Mark Legat was the sole author.'

'My father maintained that he contributed half the work in creating the book but he complained that Mark never included him in the credits when it was published with the result that they fell out and were always arguing. I understand that they ended their days in an argument and both got shot. Everybody who has read the book has died.'

Simon sat speechlessly holding his chin with his elbow on the table. He couldn't believe what he just heard.

After a long pause he said 'How did you and Cynthia meet?'

'Her husband was the architect who built the house I am now living in. He was in my original house going over the drawings for the contract on the evening he was shot chasing an intruder away from my house. He was returning that damned book which he had borrowed from my

The Illusive Diamond

father and he asked me where Mark lived. He wanted to meet him. He had the book in his pocket when he was shot.

'The man who shot him took the book from his pocket and he too was later shot. Now Cynthia. I won't even touch the book and I suggest that you get rid of it.'

Pam stayed with Simon for the rest of the week and they talked endlessly, mainly about her father and the dreaded book. She wanted to keep his mind engaged. She was seriously concerned that he was showing suicidal tendencies. She had seen these signs before and felt that the worst thing she could do now was to leave him alone. She had to keep him talking. In this situation she allowed herself to drop into lecturing mode.

'Simon' she said. 'A great deal of what we've been discussing is related to the concept of personality. In addressing this concept we are dealing with the individual and moreover a particular individual in each case. Thus, we are in an area of individual differences. Motivational variations, frustration tolerances are of major importance and have a specific effect on the way we deal with situations.

The same may be said of differences in emotional responses. Some people are more susceptible than others to emotional activation, while some adjust to emotion provoking situations in ways which are characteristic of them as individuals. One person may keep his head while another may 'blow his top'. Under comparable circumstances one may be reconciled while the other is irreconcilable. The vibrations of one, clash with the vibes of the other.

My father's vibrations were in constant confrontation with Mark Legat's, but underneath they were both decent types. In the end the book made father neurotic. His personality changed because of that book.'

Simon had been listening patiently in silence then suddenly said 'Pam, I regard myself as being responsible for the death of these people. I've thought about it long and hard.'

'Simon, it's the book that is the cause of the deaths. It started with the death of my father and has continued ever since with people dying who have had any connection with the book. The book gives off vibes that attack people's sensibilities. People have become psychotic before their death.

'Before he died my father displayed unbelievable changes in his personality. The strange thing is that he was so concerned about not being given credit in the book that was to eventually kill him.

'He presumably didn't see his name in the acknowledgements with about six other people on the back page. Perhaps that wasn't good enough for him.'

'The amazing thing is that I didn't know about all of this earlier. Ironically this makes you the legal owner of the book' Simon said shaking his head.

'Simon, I want nothing to do with the book. You can burn it as far as I am concerned.'

'Pam, we must accept that it is a work of some significance in the mining world. This talk of vibrations from a book is a bit wild.'

'Simon I want you to take that book out of my presence please. I am just not comfortable being in the same room with it. I call it vibrations but you can call it what you like, I just do not like that book. I'm not comfortable sharing my space with it.'

The next day started as usual for Simon at six. Having experienced a sleepless night Simon was still desperately tired. He was still struggling with the mental stress of the last three weeks. He played a Stravinsky tape. That was the only composer that was capable of preparing him for the day.

But not today it seemed.

Nervous and near exhaustion he was trying to clarify the situation. It was a situation that was becoming less clear by the day. It haunted him to the point of obsession.

Why were people dying around him? How does a book have vibes??

Pamela came into the kitchen and looked him squarely in the face. She sensed what she perceived as a dangerous drift towards mental breakdown.

Simon asked 'Coffee?'

'Sure' she answered.

He poured two cups and placed them on the table.

'While you're staying here with me how much is it costing you in lost income?'

'What?'

'Well roughly.'

'I qualified in psychology not accountancy. Anyway who cares.'

The Illusive Diamond

The phone on the kitchen wall began ringing. Simon took it off the hook. It was Errol in San Francisco.

'Hello Simon, just ringing to ask if you got the book.'

'Yes thanks a million Errol.'

Errol continued, 'Afraid it's something of a mess since you and I pulled it out of the water. I had to dry it before I wrapped it. That gave me time to read it. I found it very interesting reading.

'I've got a friend staying with me who works for a publishing house in New York, he's here on business for a month. He wants to speak to you at some stage about the book, when you're ready.'

'There's no development regarding Cynthia I'm afraid Simon.' They bid goodbye and hung up.

Simon turned to face Pamela. She was sitting with her head in her hands looking down at the table.

He had captured her heart weeks ago when they first met and although she had rarely left her house by the lake she had decided this time to stay with him as long as she decided he needed her. She looked up into his face lovingly. He was tall and fair and spoke with a boyish sincerity and she loved listening to him speaking even though it might be nothing of importance.

'That was Errol. The guy we stayed with in Frisco. I formed the opinion a long time ago that for Errol, caring for others is his life's work. He's a wonderful man.'

She reached up and embraced him and said, 'Like someone I know'.

CHAPTER 13

The phone started ringing. He picked it up. The voice was slow and apologetic.

'My name is Sheridan Brewster. I am staying in Errol's flat. I'm afraid I have bad news.'

'Oh dear, what can that be I wonder.' Simon assumed that Sheridan had to return to New York early. The Sheridan continued.

'Errol was run down by a truck yesterday and killed.'

'What?' Simon screamed.

'Right outside this house.' His voice broke. 'I saw it from this window. He just stepped off the kerb and the truck came round the corner and knocked him down. I ran down the stairs and when I got to him he was dead'. His voice was now practically inaudible. There was a pause. 'I called the ambulance and went to hospital with him and they confirmed he was D.O.A.'

'God!' Simon was speechless and after a long pause he said. 'That's terrible, what a ghastly thing to happen. That's awful. I hope the damn truck driver is arrested.'

Another silence as Sheridan composed himself. 'Is there anything I can do Sheridan?'

'At the moment Simon I can't get my head round the whole situation. But if I think of anything I'll let you know. Right now I aim to finish my business here and leave.

'You know Simon, Errol and his whole family were no strangers to sudden and untimely death, it seems to have been a tradition running through his family,' Sheridan said.

'Is that so, Sheridan.'

'Yes, his grandfather was shot during the twenties by claim jumpers in the Californian Gold Rush and five years ago his father fell from a fourth floor window that he was cleaning in their apartment and was impaled by the spiked railings that surrounded the basement of the block.

'Last year his mother in a shopping trip to Chicago was passing a large bank at a time when it was being raided. The gunmen were just leaving and being chased by a very brave assistant manager shouting 'Stop thief'. He was met by a hail of bullets which caused passers-by to drop to the pavement screaming. At that moment two policemen who had stopped for coffee at an adjacent café were returning to their vehicle and drew their guns returning the fire, killing one of the four gunmen.

'The last gunman of the remaining three grabbed Errol's mother, Miranda, who found herself in the middle of the shooting. Using her as a human shield he dragged her into the car. With two large gunmen and Miranda, who was of formidable proportions, it was somewhat cramped on the back seat of the Buick. At this time Miranda was suffering the inconvenience of a weak bladder and on her shopping expedition she had allowed herself to be detained by the large selection of beautiful hats on display in the millinery store for far longer than was wise.

'Miranda had allowed her bladder to become full during her inspection of the hats and it was a most inappropriate time for her to be manhandled and dragged into the back seat of a car. The vehicle sped off with Miranda into her already stretched stomach. The traumatic situation added to her personal stress and her bladder gave way.

'Unfortunately, at this time Miranda suffered a bladder infection and when the Buick reached the outskirts of the city the leader of the gang, who was sitting next to the driver, turned round to face the back and shouted 'What was that Goddam stink?'

'After a pause, Willy Shultz sitting next to Miranda shouted back 'The old bird has pissed herself and soaked the seat and me'.

"Get rid of her then for Christ's sake'.

'The driver was now doing eighty and with his eyes on the rear view mirror, mindful of the two police cars on his tail, he slowed to twenty but had no intention of stopping. Willy, recognised as a ruthless killer among his fellow gunmen because of his habit of pistol-whipping anybody for no apparent reason, leaving a trail of bodies with cracked skulls wherever he had carried out jobs, allowed the car to slow to ten miles per hour for one second, opened the door, raised his foot and kicked the unfortunate Miranda out. He slammed the door and the car sped off.

'Miranda was found by the police in pursuit, who radioed for an ambulance, and was found dead on arrival at hospital.'

'You know Simon, I loved that man like a brother. I don't know what I shall do now.

I know it's a mistake to look too far ahead but at the moment I can't see past the end of my nose.

Errol was a man of infinite writing skill and a superb artist. Even in his school days he was recognised as a skilful artist and as the years passed, he received countless awards for his children's books and his fame spread the length and breadth of California. He was becoming known right across the States. He'd recently been offered a book deal worth a million dollars and couldn't decide whether to take it. He was handsome with a finely carved profile. He had such clear skin.

He walked with a spring in his step which gave the impression that he was conceited but conceited he wasn't. He was in fact withdrawn and self-effacing. That gave some people the idea that he was lazy, which he wasn't. He was industrious.

He had an easy smile and made friends easily. He appeared to take nothing seriously. At college some teachers categorised him as lazy but at the same time they were amazed at the prodigious amount of work he produced without appearing to try. He had no interest in sport and came into class late every morning.

At his desk he appeared to be staring into space for most of the time and yet at the end of a period he produced the most spectacular work.

He never went out at night with the lads. He was always studying. Errol produced some of the most beautiful poetry and he will now never reap the benefit.'

'Sheridan I want to thank you for ringing. Take it easy old chap and ring me if there is anything I can do.' Simon hung up and looked at Pamela. She returned the look and threw her arms around his neck reading the news from his eyes that were now leaking.

'When you feel like it you can tell me' she whispered.

'You won't believe it but Errol's been killed' Simon said.

She guided him through to the sitting room sitting down on the couch together, Simon holding his head.

'I'll make you a cup of tea' she said and made her way into the kitchen.

Simon sat there looking at the floor. After a few moments Pamela brought the tea in and joined him on the couch. In an attempt to break the ice she said 'Darling, what were you about to say when the phone stopped you?'

There was a long pause while he focused his mind.

'I was about to ask you if you would like a holiday?'

'Where did you have in mind?'

'Florida or maybe Australia.'

'What gave you that idea?'

He looked at the lines on her face and said 'Just lately I've been thinking that you're looking tired.'

She looked pensive and bit her lip, then she asked 'Simon, how was he killed?'

He had walked over to the window and was looking out. Without turning round he answered 'He was run down by a truck.'

'Oh my God!' Her hand went up and covered her mouth.

He was standing with his back to her, looking into the distance, his hands in his pockets. The sun was bright the snow was cold and crisp reflecting the whiteness.

He turned to face her, his face stern and serious. She stepped towards him. They embraced in silence. After a long pause Simon said 'The journey through life consists of many stages and we must pass through each one before passing on to the next. This process makes us stronger and more able to face up to the further challenges of life.'

'That is very true Simon. Are you feeling stronger after your recent experiences?'

'I completed the last stage when I stopped looking for Cynthia and I can handle this last episode without much of a problem.'

She reached up and kissed him gently on the cheek and turned and they walked back to the couch.

As soon as they were seated he took her face in both hands and said 'Pamela,' he looked closely at her face, she looked grey, 'I've been worried about you. You look very tired. You need a rest. You've been under pressure worrying about me and Cynthia.'

'I suppose it can be said that is true of both of us' she said, 'I suppose we both need a holiday'.

The Illusive Diamond

The call that Pamela was making was her last one before returning to Simon's house. She had been away for three days staying at her own house and she was looking forward to seeing Simon.

This call was to the mental home at which she'd been visiting patients for ten years.

It was a cold, bright, sunny morning and as was her habit she entered the private room of this morning's patient from the garden, walking along the paths of the beautifully manicured grounds inspecting the flowerbeds. She watched the patients wandering around as if they were lost. She felt she identified with them more than with the people out in the street. She felt that she should be with them permanently because this is where she was needed.

Her patient, Jennifer Burgess, met her at the double doors and closed them as soon as she'd entered to keep the heat in. 'I'm not sure you should have made the trip today Pamela. You don't look well. But I must confess that I do look forward to your visits' she said as they both sat down in the soft armchairs. Jennifer looked deeply into Pamela's face. 'No dear you don't look at all well.'

'Oh that'll pass it's only the weather. I just had to see you Jenny. How have you been keeping?'

'Oh I'm OK but I think they've brought more spies in to watch us.'

Pam laughed and was reminded of Jennifer's habit of polishing a silver spoon whilst she talked.

When she returned to Simon's house she found he was out. She walked through to the study and found a note on his desk. It said that he had been called up to the mining camp at Great Bear Lake. He was taking a flight from Selkirk and would be back tonight.

She left the note where it was and walked back to the kitchen where she began making coffee. She put the water on to boil and then turned to her briefcase, took out a pile of paperwork and spread it on the table in order of priority.

She made the coffee poured it, sat at the table and began working. The work consisted of reports on all her patients that she had seen in the last three days.

Simon had left early that morning after a call from Mac at the camp the night before. When he'd arrived at the airport he was informed that all flights north and north west were being held back for at least two hours due to bad weather moving in. Cloud was low and there were snow storms around Prince Albert that were moving south making visibility extremely poor. This was confirmed by the weather bureau where he complained that he could have been informed before he left home when he booked his place.

The result was that Simon was forced to hang around Selkirk airport. He ate a hearty breakfast washed down with a gallon of coffee and read the morning paper.

He looked around at the group waiting to join him on the plane. There were half a dozen miners returning from leave. A group of adult students from Columbia University with their professor completing a tour of mining camps and now returning to their college. There was a father taking his wife and two young children back to Vancouver after visiting relations in Winnipeg.

The miners were clearly used to this waiting around, it was to be expected when travelling by plane in temperatures such as these. They lived and worked in the same climate all their lives and had nothing to discuss. They just sat around in the plastic armchairs and dozed.

The adult students were full of excitement about their trip which was coming to an end and they now harboured concerns about utilising the acquired knowledge in the forthcoming examinations. They chatted incessantly about what they had seen and learnt so far and made notes as they reminded each other of certain aspects of particular visits.

Their professor sat alone with a furrowed brow, doubt showing on his lined forehead. Should he utilise this waiting time by squeezing in another visit to a small mining complex that he knew was in the vicinity. They could reach it by bus which travelled the route and went straight to the property. They could catch the next plane.

The professor's name was Crammer. He was Crammer by name and crammer by nature. He was known among the students for his habit of cramming as much into a session as he could. Not a minute of tuition time was wasted and he was highly regarded by the Board of Governors, but he was overlooked on last year's round of promotions once again because he was known as a ditherer and was incapable of making decisions quickly. He spent most of his time worrying.

The professor was a geologist and had published many papers on the subject. He'd read everything there was to read on the subject and was a recognised genius.

The professor was the product of the college at which he was currently employed having returned after twenty years. He wore a green suit with brown flecks in it that looked as if it had been knitted with dead grass. A brown bow tie and suede shoes with crepe soles put him in a league of his own. A habit of looking at the ceiling when speaking, he caused a great deal of humour among the students. It was a common supposition around the college that he was servicing the music teacher Miss Boneshaft.

The father with the family, Thomas, was worried about the flight postponement because it would delay his return to work and that is something that would not go down well with sales management at the office. It might even jeopardise his employment. They were looking for excuses to terminate people because sales had plunged dramatically.

He had taken the family on this trip against his better judgement to please his wife who wanted the children to attend the birthday party of her sister's youngest. He wasn't keen on the idea because it meant taking time off work. Also her sister had an older child who had a birthday coming up in a month's time and they would be expected to attend that one too.

Thomas was a sales representative and he had been with the company Wellington Soft Drinks for ten years. His sales had dropped lately in fact turnover in the company generally was down. It was clear that a reduction in staff was inevitable. He was not at all comfortable with the delayed flight, in fact he was decidedly unhappy with his present position.

Suddenly the public address system burst into life and his flight was announced. Passengers were asked to make their way to the departure gate as the crew of the aeroplane passed through the gate onto the tarmac carrying their little black leather briefcases. They walked with a confident military spring in their step as they passed out into the clear blue sky that shone down over the tarmac.

The passengers struggled to their feet, gathered their hand baggage and made their way over to the gate. Thomas's wife Claudia ushered her family gently along preoccupied with thoughts that were otherwise engaged. She was confident that Thomas's job was secure but she could not tell him. She had been involved in an affair with the MD of the company since the last shake up the company had about two years ago. At that time they made five salesmen redundant and she saved Thomas's job by making herself available to the MD on Tuesday and Thursday lunchtimes. Since that time Thomas had experienced rapid promotion and was under the impression that it was his business acumen that had achieved the meteoric rise in salary but she knew it was her talent.

Things had grown much worse in the company now and she didn't think she could maintain the momentum that had so far secured his position on the company ladder. However, she could only try, but there is no way that she could tell her husband that she had made his position more secure than anyone else's on the company.

Eventually the plane took off into clear blue skies. They hadn't been flying for long when they met a snowstorm. The pilot pulled the nose up to get above it and achieved some success. The snow thinned but not for long and soon returned in full bodied opacity filling the screen in a blanket of white. Increasing height reduced visibility even more so he dropped down looking for some clear sky.

Pushing the plane down he watched the altimeter, it was going round and round as if it was out of control. He entered dense cloud and then clear sky. Suddenly he saw roads and hills in clear daylight but he was too low for comfort. He pulled the column back and climbed a thousand feet and flew straight for a while, watching the altimeter. Even flying straight the thing was going crazy. He hit more cloud and snow and a fierce wind picked up buffeting the plane which began sliding to starboard.

He dropped down again and broke through the low level cloud immediately meeting clear weather again, but once again finding the ground was close and the altimeter told him nothing. He gritted his teeth and pulled back on the column again and the metal bird screamed upwards once more. The snow turned to rain and then a mixture of both. Visibility was poor and the cabin filled with dismayed shouts from the cabin staff. He levelled out and watching the altimeter decided that the thing was useless he planned on a measured drop which he could arrest easily when meeting clear weather.

The plane. A DE HAVILAND CANADA DASH 8, had thirty six seats and was only about half full. All conversation stopped as the engines demanded sound space 'til it levelled out, then chatting began again. The students became immediately engrossed in deep conversation until a chap who appeared as their spokesman, by the name of Steve Benning, suddenly spoke above the other voices and delivered his question towards the professor.

'Professor Crammer' he called along the row of seats.

'Yes Benning?'

The Illusive Diamond

'When we complete our time at University and we achieve our degrees should we have need to worry about job prospects?'

There was a pause as their leader considered the question.

'Mr Benning, as I've explained to the class on many occasions, there is no reason for you to be concerned about employment prospects. The world is your oyster. Geologists are in great demand all over the industrialised world.'

'What positions do you favour for us professor?' Benning asked.

'The choice is yours. There is a multitude of positions in industry and of course there is always teaching.'

Benning yawned and continued talking to the fellow student next to him.

Among the books he had read the professor regarded THE ILLUSIVE DIAMOND as the most authoritative. He always told his students to acquire a copy from the cheap bookshop in town close to the university and to study it.

The ferocious weather moved relentlessly south to Winnipeg and beyond and Pamela looking out of the window was conscious that Simon could well be in a plane in this weather.

She thought long and hard. Could it be possible that a plane would take off in this weather. She covered her eyes. No never she thought.

She stood motionless before the window her tall elegant figure outlined by the white expanse of the endless snowscape outside.

She decided to phone the Selkirk airport. She got through to the information desk after endless delays and was told that visibility had improved and the flight had taken off. The current conditions had developed since the plane moved further north. In fact the plane should be experiencing clear weather at this moment. Unfortunately radio contact had been lost due to the storm.

Pamela returned to her paperwork more than a little concerned. Simon should never have gone today.

While she was visiting her patients she diverted to call on her area chief to discuss a particular patient. He had observed how ill she looked and that she needed a rest. She promised to take one. As she was thinking of this meeting she relaxed against the back of the high backed chair she was sitting in at Simon's desk. She looked at the ceiling. She was aware of being worried but in truth she was sick with fear. Looking at the window the weather looked to be getting worse.

Steven Benning was twenty five years old and something of a trouble maker. He was facetious and cynical but he possessed a very sharp brain. He achieved a first in every subject at college and was regarded as a golden boy by all the teaching staff. Even at senior school his potential was noted.

His parents were very rich and contributed to every cause that the head decided was necessary for the college.

Misdemeanours, which were many, always seemed to be overlooked or regarded as boyish pranks or mistakes on the young Benning's part.

He was generally regarded as one of the educationally elite and was bound to do well in anything he undertook in life. He was also a poseur and currently drove to college in a Ferrari.

In his teens he had left more than one young female pregnant that his father was obliged to buy off. By the time he was twenty one he had a pilot's licence, had owned two planes and crashed them both.

His father's occupation was the purchase of companies from which he sold off non-earning sections. He modernised the production base and the distribution network then put the whole thing on the market again. Benning's father was a millionaire. He had served bravely during the war and received a medal for his bravery. He was a different person when he came home.

In 1940 he was called up into the army and placed in the British Expeditionary to France. He was among the first British troops to land on French soil. They landed at Cherbourg and as the ship pulled away to return to the UK a train loaded with German soldiers unloaded at Cherbourg station and rounded up the dumfounded British and put them on a train to Germany where they worked in the salt mines in Silesia. They'd been taken prisoner without firing a shot.

He soon escaped and with another Englishman headed west. All they were able to take with them was a little German bread.

Early in the journey they came across a women's prison camp. The inmates were terribly emaciated, their eyes dark and sunken and most were bald. They were trying to climb the wire, crying and screaming.

The sight reduced the two men to a state of utter devastation as they could do nothing to relieve the situation. They had to leave as quickly as possible feeling totally helpless.

The following day they came across another group. This time it was teenagers, about fifty of them, living and working in a camp of wooden

The Illusive Diamond

huts making clothes for German soldiers. The two stayed a while to scrounge some food and get directions and then moved on.

They made their way through France jumping on freight trains, finally arriving in Le Havre where they stole a small fishing boat during the night. After two days, during which they didn't think the little engine would make it, they landed on Brighton beach. They were interrogated and returned to their regiments.

The French boat was smuggling wine, champagne and gauloises which was to be exchanged with the contents of an English boat carrying Scotch whisky, America gaberdine and nylons. The trade was a monthly occurrence at the same compass bearing and the Frenchmen were on edge if they had to hang round for more than a moment or two in sight of the German guns. They searched the Englishmen's boat speaking in whispers, and let them pass.

When Benning was returned to his regiment it was found that he had a natural affinity with a rifle. He had never handled a gun before joining the Gloucester Regiment and upon discovering his talent he was promptly sent up to Scotland to live in the wild with instructions to live only on what he could shoot.

Bennng's family were farmers and like all his family he was a man of the soil. After a fortnight in Scotland he returned to his camp in the south better fed than his comrades.

He was made the company sniper, given his own quarters and was required to spend every day acquainting himself with all the latest weaponry available.

Suddenly he was respected by officers and men alike and promotion came quickly. Soon he displayed a sergeant's stripes on his uniform. A secretive person never known to show emotion but on this occasion a slight indication of pride could be detected as everyone in his barrack room crowded round to congratulate him on receipt of his third stripe.

He hadn't been back long when he was put in charge of a newly formed Bren gun company. A squad of four men were given a Bren gun carrier, a lightweight open topped vehicle suitable for driving on made up roads only.

It carried a crew of four men, two Bren guns, a dozen boxes of ammunition and a week's rations for four men. The vehicle was no bigger than a jeep it was very limited in its use.

A company of men, thirty two in all, were given eight vehicles and sent up to the Yorkshire moors where they lived and trained for a month, learning to service the vehicle along with the Bren gun, until they knew the vehicle inside and out.

They spent a few days training in landing barges on the beaches in Devon until they were to find out what they were training for.

Eventually they were included in a raid on Ostend with a battalion of Canadian infantry. The exercise was basically to test the German defences.

They loaded their vehicles onto cruisers and towing their barges they set off for France. Halfway across the Channel they climbed aboard their barges with their vehicles and completed the remainder of the journey to the beach.

They disembarked, loaded their supplies onto the carriers and set off in a convoy of eight carriers moving inland. They had been driving for forty five minutes when they made the first contact with German opposition. It was when an 88mm shell hit the first carrier in the convoy.

A second shell hit Benning's vehicle and took off the front wheel left side and the vehicle rocked and slid slowly into a roadside ditch. Benning was thrown against the side of the angled vehicle with men and supplies landing on top of him.

The carriers to the rear crashed one into another perfecting an ambush that was clearly a well advised plan. The narrow road was completely blocked with all the carriers stationary behind the lead vehicle and at the mercy of the gunners.

Cannon fire continued until all the carriers were crippled. The 88s were joined by mortars and machine guns and the noise was deafening. Men were screaming everywhere. Benning was choking with the smoke of burning tyres, flesh and fuel. Bodies were falling on top of him. He felt the warmth of liquid as his uniform became soaked with blood from the bodies lying on top of him. He began to consider the possibility of suffocating under the weight on top of him.

This was his first taste of a real battle and he was terrified. His vehicle took another hit and the weight which had smothered him was removed. He was able to breathe and he did with some relief, but was he injured? Had he been hit?

He moved his arms then his legs. He wiggled his toes then his fingers. He opened his eyes in the now thinning smoke. He ran his hands over his body to check if he was in one piece. He could not believe

The Illusive Diamond

he had not been hit. He would have to move from this position before he choked from the putrid smoke.

He shouted 'Let's get out of here' but there was no movement from the bodies around him. He heard German voices. He had to decide whether to play dead and lie still and suffocate inhaling the choking smoke or put his hands up.

He chose the latter. He struggled to his feet and was confronted by a long line of German soldiers checking the vehicles for signs of life.

He was instructed to climb out of the vehicle and up onto the road where he was searched. He was placed into a lorry with six other survivors and transported to Stalag 43 in Germany.

On arrival they were given their first meal which was macaroni. As soon as he arrived at the camp Benning considered the possibility of escape having studied the route in and did his best to memorise it. He also began picking up the remarks made by the guards in an effort to learn German.

He became friends with a fellow Englishman Arthur Legg who said he was keen to escape since in the last letter he received at camp his wife said she was pregnant. Arthur was a friendly chap with a great sense of humour, seeing something funny in everything.

Over the next few days and weeks they discussed the plans for their escape.

It was whilst marching with a working party outside the camp that they planned the escape. They saw that the number of guards reduced at that time. At just such a time they were able to take advantage. Both fell down and rolled into a ditch at the side of the road and waited for the marching column to pass.

They lay there 'til it felt safe and then cautiously got up. After walking through most of the night they took shelter in a bombed building and got some sleep. They were woken in the late morning by voices. Peeping through a hole in the bricks they saw a group of farm workers both men and women, working in a nearby field. They decided to approach them and find out where they were and try to scrounge some food.

Entering the squeaking five bar gate they closed it behind them and made their way over to the workers. The noise of the gate attracted the attention of all the workers who looked up as one. Their gaze was drawn past the two Englishmen as the gate squeaked once more.

The two POWs turned to see who the extra visitor was. They were depressed to see it was two German soldiers who immediately shouted 'Halt!'

The two Englishmen stopped and put their hands up. The Germans had their rifles pointing at them and closed in asking if they were Polish.

Benning shouted quickly 'Nein! English!' knowing that the Germans thought little of the Poles.

'English?' the surprised German questioned.

'Ja.'

The Germans gripped their rifles in a more businesslike manner and went into earnest conversation.

Benning assumed they were asked where did they come from in German and answered in English that they were escaped POWs. The soldiers sent for an officer. The English friends thought that this was the end and prepared for the worst.

The officer arrived and after a muffled conversation with the soldiers approached the POWs smiling, presumably thinking the two were not who they said they were. He spoke in perfect English.

'Where in England do you come from?'

The two were flabbergasted by his English and answered his questions. When the interrogation was completed the officer took them to the canteen in the German camp. It was just a wooden barn with a soldier making tea. The officer ordered tea and buns for them both, pushed an apple in their pockets and practised his English which he said was going rusty. He had attended school in Rugby before the war and was proud of it.

He told them that he was going to send them to a POW camp not far from where they were at the moment, it was full of Australians so they should be comfortable. He put them on a lorry and off they went.

They were there in thirty minutes. He was correct. The camp was full of Aussies and every one of them had an escape plan. The guards were very lax and it was obvious that they were not disciplined soldiers because escape was a daily occurrence. The place was more like holiday camp.

Benning and his friend joined two Australians to make their escape. The party moved very quickly from the area and had soon crossed the border into France where they met up with a group of Free French and worked with them raiding German arms dumps and knocking off high ranking German officers.

They quite enjoyed the work feeling they were doing something useful. The Frenchmen promised to get hem to UK when their next delivery came from the UK.

They took part in blowing up a train from Germany one day and the following day they blew up a bridge. In the evening they were told that an RAF plane was to be met bringing medical supplies in the middle of the night and they were to help with torches, after which they could get on it for the return journey.

They were over the moon. That evening the whole team sat listening to the radio for the coded messages from the BBC which would give them the time and place of the landing.

On a cloud-free moonlight night at the appointed time they gathered in a field and hid in the places they were told and waited for the sound of a plane.

Within five minutes of the arranged time the plane was above them and the whole party lined up with their lit torches to form a landing path. The CUB landed comfortably and the team threw the supplies off in double quick time. The two Englishmen and the two Aussies climbed aboard, the path was lit again and the CUB took off in five minutes. The whole operation was carried out with hardly a word being spoken.

They landed in England and after interrogation went straight to the nearest bar.

Walter Benning returned to France on D-Day and won a VC. He had sent a Bren gun team up the beach to deal with a pillbox that was holding up progress with its 88mm.

On arrival at their firing position the two men were immediately pinned down by a hail of rifle fire from four directions.

Benning waited for them to produce some results with no success. He filled his pockets with grenades he ran up the beach to where the two men were lying. He found that both were wounded. He ran up to the pillbox below the gun slit and lobbed his grenade through the aperture. Running back to the two men he grabbed them both by their collars and dragged them down the beach to the waiting medics.

He had identified the positions from where the rifle fire was coming and picked up his own rifle and dealt with all four positions. Then he pressed his men forward. It was that action for which he was awarded the VC.

Three months after demobilisation his parents died. The time spent in the services had brought about a change in his personality. He was no longer the man of the soil he was now more aware of the business side of life and toil on the farm did not form part of it. Success did not come from feeding pigs.

He sold the farm to a developer and bought a run down fifty bedroom seaside hotel, refurbished it and sold it making a very interesting profit. He then bought a one hundred bedroom hotel in Brighton, refurbished it and sold it also at an interesting profit. Thus he moved into the world of business. Property business.

He bought a company that manufactured paint. The company was founded in 1860 and was very run down like all the staff. He inspected the company property and found that apart from the main factory and office building there was a lot of disused buildings rambling over countless acres of land with no connection with the paint industry at all. He set about disposing of these derelict buildings in separate parcels.

He discovered that the company had been very well connected around the world before the War and set about re-establishing those connections and secured a distribution network.

He modernised the factory and the production base. He refurbished the offices and replaced most of the staff including the management. He took on a managing director and promised him a nice bonus if he doubled the turnover in twelve months.

At the end of one year he had doubled the orders for the next two years. Benning paid him his bonus and put the company on the market. He had made his first million.

From then on he spent his life buying and selling companies eventually becoming a multimillionaire.

CHAPTER 14

Benning met his wife Susan in London. They met at a book launching in Knightsbridge. The book was on business management by a mutual friend. Benning had invited her for a drink afterwards.

She had told herself that there was nothing like a common interest to promote bonding. It might've been wise to say goodbye and leave, instead she agreed and by the time they finally parted she knew where the friendship was going. She would never allow a friendship to develop without feeling she was in control, but she couldn't be sure about this one.

Susan was in London on business, buying clothes for her women's shops in Vancouver. She took Benning back with her where they married.

In Vancouver Benning suggested that she start a chain of women's shops in conjunction with a chain of men's shops. The idea was to come to fruition sooner than expected when the shop adjacent to her existing women's shop became vacant and she created her first men's store.

London at that time was the world centre for both men's and women's clothes and Susan was now able to buy the best of both on her trips to London. The Canadians were overcome by the standard of the clothes and her shops became very successful. But further plans for expansion were put on hold with the arrival of their son.

However Walter continued to study the stockbroker columns to add to his portfolio.

Visibility improved in patches and the pilot gently reduced height.

Suddenly a clearing occurred and through the thinning snow cloud he found that he was flying parallel to a road. The telephone poles in the hedges blurred into a line of Burnt Umber by the speed of the plane. A flock of birds rose en masse from a field frightened by the sudden roar of the engine. One flew straight into the plane and was instantly dispatched, a ball of feathers.

The pilot pulled the nose up a little and levelled out. The engineer was studying the maps and giving the pilot navigation. Through a clearing the pilot saw a railway line and shouted the news to him.

'Follow it!' came the reply.

'If I see it for long enough' the pilot responded.

The plane bucked and rocked violently and began to lose height gain. Suddenly the roof of the large farmhouse appeared closer than it should be forcing the pilot to bank sharply to the right. Dense woods appeared momentarily as they made height. Leaves from the trees were sent fluttering first up then down forming a kaleidoscope of colour with the snowflakes as the aircraft swept over. The pilot pulled the nose up and ran into more cloud and snow as the engines screamed in protest.

Simon looked out of the window at the increased noise and caught a glimpse of a herd of cattle as they galloped in panic at the sudden roar.

The pilot continued to climb in search of visibility. He shook his head. 'We should never have left the ground today' he said to the Engineer.

The pilot applied a little forward pressure on the stick and some light pressure on the right pedal making a gentle descending turn. Both the pilot and the aeroplane were under stress but both were performing admirably showing perfect control of the pitch, roll and yaw. The plane was twisting and shaking and the occasional bump punctuated the turbulence. The wind was screaming and the wing tips were covered in ice. The windows were partially covered in snow and the reflection from the windows gave the atmosphere in the cabin a strange luminosity.

They were now flying totally on instruments with a faulty altimeter. The navigator was concentrating on his ground mapping radar and hoping for a break in the cloud so that he might fix their location visually.

As the plane shuddered once more the flight attendant came through the cockpit door.

'Some of the customers are becoming violently sick Captain' she said.

The ghostly half light was broken with bright white flashes and total

The Illusive Diamond

concentration allowed no response from the pilot except 'I'm not surprised'.

Years of practice that qualified the man for his job made him cool under pressure, but he began to feel he was losing the race.

The aeroplane shuddered as the weather continued to pound them. Violent jolts shook them testing the strength of the aircraft. Their harnesses cut into their shoulders as the captain fought to keep control.

Suddenly the turbulence ceased and visibility improved to such an extent that they actually caught a glimpse of the sun, but only momentarily. The sudden strong light gave a sharp definition to features on the ground. The captain could see the shadows of rocky outcrops clearly marking the snow covered ground.

The navigator recognised identifiable landmarks in the sudden boost of light and marked his maps accordingly.

'We're off course Skipper' he shouted.

'How far?'

'We're at least ten miles too far south.'

The captain attempted to rectify the situation and pulled the plane to the right but the high wind started up again and the plane began slipping sideways to the left and would not be held back.

Captain Jessop had been flying for twenty years. He was a fighter pilot in the Royal Canadian Air Force before he came into civil aviation. He flew helicopters in Vietnam where he ferried ordinance or troops and lifted transport out of the deep snow in their winter storm.

He was reminded of just such a storm, similar to this present one, which was very common in Vietnam. The wind was vicious, just like today's.

On a typical mission to pick up wounded he had landed in a snowstorm and was immediately pinned down by small arms fire. It took two hours to pick up the wounded and the soldiers carrying the casualties out to the chopper sustained three more casualties.

Eventually, he was able to lift off having carried one man on his back crawling on all fours and subsequently subdued the Chinese attack on the plane with his own sidearm and his co-pilot's skill on the machine gun.

Ferrying casualties was a hell of a job especially in winter. On his last trip he was sent to pick up two men in a deep jungle position. He landed in a clearing and the Chinese spotted him as he touched down and opened up. The team he was meeting could not get out to him. Jessop and his co-pilot opened up with the machine gun and sidearm and Jessop ran with two stretchers across the clearing to the thick bush.

Cutting his way through the thick bamboo and dense greenery he reached the squad of men that were waiting for him and between them they strapped the wounded to the stretchers.

At that point the Chinese had discovered where they were and directed their fire at their position. They were blasted with mortars and grenades and Jessop picked up a shrapnel wound in the shoulder. Even so he managed to carry one end of a stretcher back to the clearing.

The Chinese knew what was being done and when they reached the clearing they were met with a hail of fire. Grenades and mortars were hurled at the chopper.

They watched the chopper disintegrate before their eyes as the concentrated Chinese fire did its work while they stood at the edge of the clearing.

As if in satisfaction the firing suddenly stopped. Tony Jessop took advantage of the pause and ran over to the wreck. He climbed inside and the shell was immediately showered by automatic fire. He looked around for sensitive equipment or weapons that were undamaged that might be useful to the enemy. If he couldn't remove them he would have to destroy them.

All the time he was crawling about in the craft it was subjected to bullets pinging off the shell and some coming through showering the inside with plastic and metal.

What equipment was working he smashed with his pistol or put a round into it then, at a suitable moment, he ran like mad, back to the bushes ducking the light rifle fire that came his way. He threw himself into the lush greenery and turned to return some fire with his pistol. He lay there close to one of the soldiers who carried a stretcher with him.

The soldier threw him an M14 and a belt of 7.62mm ammo. It had belonged to one of the injured men he said. 'It will be more use to you than yours' the soldier shouted. Incoming shots kicked up the earth as Tony Jessop found the rifle infinitely more useful at that range, than his pistol. When he hit a man with a shot from it the man went down. He was in a bad position and radioed for another chopper with a medic on board. One of his casualties was in excruciating pain and he should get the boy back ASAP.

They dropped back into thicker cover to wait for the chopper.

They lay quietly in the dense jungle listening intently for the sound of a chopper. Tony Jessop squatted behind a rock pile nursing the worst of the wounded as bullets punctured the undergrowth around him.

Soon they heard the unmistakable flapping of helicopter rotors and Jessop ran towards the clearing. His movement brought a fresh outburst of automatic fire in his direction. He reached the clearing as the backup chopper made a pass over the wrecked craft. He punched numbers into his radio and described his exact position attempting to make visual contact with the pilot. He succeeded. But as the bird closed in, automatic gunfire was ranged against it. The plane hovered over the scene as the co-pilot tried to pick off the gun men with his machine gun through the open door.

Fire from the ground increased and Jessop could hear the pilot cursing over the radio as he attempted to avoid the shower of bullets coming through the skin. He was performing acrobatics in his efforts to reach the ground. The closer he got the more the firepower increased. He was now taking cannon fire.

The rescue chopper called for extra support, there was no possibility of him landing here without some heavy backup. Jessop ran back to his wounded men and reported the situation to the crew who were keeping up sustained fire from their position.

The sergeant decided that when the second chopper arrived he would bring up the heavy mortars. This was no longer a little skirmish it had become serious and the casualties were suffering. They had to be taken out.

The Chinese had smelt a rat and intended to come in for the kill. Their manpower had increased. What was originally a patrol out to search the area was now a full blown attack force. They had realised that they had run into a base camp. What they didn't know was that it was a medical supply base with insignificant ordinance.

They had brought up reinforcements and they were now using mortars and cannon fire. They meant business.

Jessop called his base camp and confirmed the need for assistance. His casualties had to be moved and he was unable to move them. He needed heavy backup to clear the Chinese from the area.

'A helicopter gun ship is in your area and can be with you in five minutes' came the reply.

Almost as estimated a gunship appeared on the horizon, bristling with armament. He hovered over the wreckage and greeted Jessop on the radio confirming the position of the enemy. Then he let go with everything as the first chopper with gun blazing lowered gently to the ground sheltering behind the wreckage. The enemy area went quiet and Jessop called for the wounded to be brought up. He threw the worst casualty over his shoulder and carried him out to the waiting plane then ran back for another. In all he got five wounded on the plane then climbed in himself screaming 'Let's go driver' and then set about attending to the wounded.

The helicopter left the ground no more than five feet when they heard a resounding crack and the plane fell back to earth. It landed fairly softly at the point where it had just left.

The pilot screamed 'We've just lost two rotor blades!'

There was a chorus of 'For Christ's sake' and 'Son of a bitch' or similar shouts as Jessop grabbed the machine gun from its mounting in the doorway and in the shadow of the plane he blasted away at the area where the Chinese were last seen.

The pilot radioed the backup plane hovering above. That pilot had already seen their predicament and was already on his way down. Jessop guided him down as he continued to blast away at any potential movement.

The medic continued to work furiously on his patients in the downed plane. The third plane landed successfully and return fire had all but ceased but it had to stay that way while they moved the wounded onto the third plane. Jessop kept watch on the Chinese line as this was done and they all climbed aboard on completion. Space was limited and the chopper struggled to get off the ground with the extra weight. Tony Jessop became giddy as the pain grew unbearable. His head began to spin. His leg reminded him that there was a slug buried in the flesh.

A combination of shock and loss of blood had left him very weak and he passed out. Blood was caked around a shrapnel wound in his shoulder and the medic saw it and gave him a shot of morphine. On inspection the medic saw that the bullet in the leg had entered one side of the calf muscle and passed out of the other and had not broken the bone. He applied a dressing and did the same to the shoulder.

Jessop ground his teeth and patted his shoulder as he remembered that day. He had received a medal for his part in the action and he shook his head when he thought of it.

He was saddened when he reflected on the damage the war in Vietnam had wrought on that beautiful country. It would eventually grow again it's true but it was so sad that these little harmless people should be so traumatised by other people's disagreement. He shook his head again.

His mind was drawn back to the storm in the Canadian countryside and his problem with handling the plane in today's storm.

The meteorological office needed reorganising if it had no information on this storm. He should never have left the ground. He scanned the wings and the engines. The starboard engine was cutting out and feathering then starting again. There was a build up of ice on the leading edge of both wings. Things weren't looking good.

If he ever managed to land this kite he would have it condemned. He would make sure that it never flew again.

Simon had flown through bad weather but had never experienced anything as bad as this.

He wondered if Pamela had come home yet. She had looked ill lately, what could the cause be, he asked himself. He would ring home as soon as he landed.

The plane was being buffeted by high winds and was rocking furiously. It was sliding from one side to the other. How the hell does a pilot fly the thing in such conditions, Simon asked himself.

He wondered what Mac's real reason was for wanting him up there. They had talked vaguely about directorships and he suspected that Mac wanted to bring in a friend or relation. That was OK as far as Simon was concerned. He didn't want his position in the company any longer. He'd be happy to stand down. He didn't want responsibility any longer. Even if that wasn't the reason for the meeting he would still stand down.

The plane hit an air pocket and dropped twenty feet. Simon was left in the air as the seat dropped, stretching the safety strap to its limit, cutting into him.

The pilot's voice came over the loudspeakers informing the passengers that he was planning to land at the nearest airstrip which was McMurry. Everyone took a sigh of relief and cheered ecstatically.

The plane had left Selkirk at two thirty and it was now evening. It was dark outside. Simon wiped the window with his hand but could make out nothing because of the bright lights in the cabin. A ninety minute flight had taken half a day. He exhaled between clenched teeth.

He slipped further down into the high backed chair and folded his arms across his chest. Closing his eyes he tried to sleep. He thought of Pamela and her theory of the vibes, in particular the vibes given off by the book that killed everyone who read it. He shook his head and smiled. The girl must be crazy.

The plane was now covered in thick snow and the sound of the engines was muffled by the thick coating over each unit. This created the effect that they were gliding through a lace curtain. Inside the passenger cabin all was quiet save for the muffled sobs from a young woman at the back of the plane. Up front, a solitary vicar, his head bent forward was muttering to himself. Each occupant was clinging to his or her partner.

In the pilot's cabin the pilot was tapping the altimeter as he spoke to the engineer. 'We must be over McMurray now, I'll drop down. Keep your eyes peeled.'

With the thick snow falling the windscreen wipers were struggling to do their job. The two men searched the exterior darkness frantically from the windows on all sides of the cabin, their faces close to the glass as the pilot gently lowered the plane.

Suddenly, the engineer shouted 'We've passed the airfield and we're heading for Birch Mountain. Pull up!'

She looked wistfully out of the window. She wasn't afraid for herself. She was afraid that death would take everyone close to her and leave her completely alone. The thought of losing Simon was paralysing her with fear. Death was not her enemy. Her enemy was fear. The fear of being left alone as she was when she was a child.

Having been left alone for hours when she was twelve years old in the empty house her father would come home and come to her room and make her perform weird tricks and do those strange things. After being alone for so long she was happy to see him and was pleased to do his bidding.

Only in maturity had she realised the depravity of what she was obliged to do and had kept it to herself resulting in the inability to recognise her own sexuality, until she met Simon. There was no escape from the turmoil inflicted on the mind by the emotions.

Standing in the white light reflected from the window she watched the fierce storm blowing outside the house and tried to assess the energy in such ferocity.

Such energy was boiling inside her and Simon was not here to sooth away the pain she was feeling. The hurt was still there and the tragedy of her father's abuse of her had resurfaced in Simon's absence. The pain of being alone and Simon being on a plane in this ghastly weather. The inability to vent her feelings caused her to cover her eyes and she walked through to the bedroom sobbing.

She was so unhappy without him. She threw herself on the bed and buried her face in the pillow. After ten minutes she rolled over onto her back and looked up at the ceiling, thinking of Simon and the weather. She'd had no news of him. She sat upright and throwing her legs over the side of the bed she stepped into her slippers. She returned to the sitting room and another window.

She watched the storm, which had not abated, and after a moment was aware of the yellow stained book with curled up pages on the half round table in front of her.

She saw that the front cover was missing and she absentmindedly picked up the book and quickly flicked through the stained pages as she twitched her nose. She arrived at the back page then she saw what it was. It was the copy of THE ILLUSIVE DIAMOND that was retrieved from the sea.

She stormed out of the room and into the kitchen throwing the book into the garbage bin. The tragedy of her father's book and his abuse resurfaced and if Simon brought the book into the house again he would cause another tragedy – between them. The hurt was still there and resurfaced in the shape of the slamming of the kitchen door as she returned to the sitting room.

She returned to the study, to the desk. She sat at the typewriter looking out of the window watching the snow build up in the garden. Watched it hang from the branches of the trees and drape from the twigs like a curtain. Totally immersed in the scene with which she connected Simon she forgot the report she had been building since earlier in the day.

The view was so pretty. Everything was pretty. It was quite natural that Simon should be part of this whole scene. It was bound to happen. She had always been part of it but she didn't realise how lucky she was until she met Simon.

Now she had become part of a personal scene that she had never planned, never wanted. She had been perfectly happy, living alone, involved with her work and her friends, contributing to her professional magazine, lecturing her students. Then Simon happened. She could hate him for destroying her life. Now she was in turmoil. She knew how much she loved him. He had that stupid boyish grin that made her go weak at the knees. Now, he'd gone on that damned plane in this weather. He was so infuriating.

She folded her arms on the desk top and dropped her head down on to them and howled loudly.

Through the break in the clouds the pilot saw that they were flying in a valley. On his left he could see the blue black tips of the Lower Birch Range and on his right the foothills of the Great Birch mountain. Through the thickening mist he could just make out that he was heading straight for the side of the massive Great Birch rising sheer out of the snow to a height of one thousand feet. Snowflakes created a curtain of white across the screen.

The glistening white cone surrounded by a sinister swirl of cloud hovering just a few metres from the blue craggy peak presented a solid white wall directly across his front.

He was pulling on the column with all his strength. The engines were screaming as the craggy white wall came closer. The plane was standing on its tail now fighting against the force of gravity.

Simon, woken by the vibration passing through the body of the plane and the screaming of the engines was immediately aware that they were in trouble. Through his window he could see the angle of ascent by the passing mist.

Small articles of personal baggage slid past him down the aisle towards the back of the plane as the angle of the plane asserted itself. It was clear to Simon that it would all come back in the opposite direction when the angle of flight was rectified.

The few females in the cabin screamed, some in a subdued manner, others quite loudly. One or two men shouted blasphemously some grabbed their fellow passenger. Most were frightened. Simon said a silent prayer.

Pamela was feeling happy today. She had been singing all the morning. She was singing when she heard a knock at the door. What a time for a visitor when she was working on the place to make it look nice for Simon's homecoming. She couldn't have visitors this morning.

She flung open the door to find two policemen standing outside. She looked at them and frowned.

'Yes?'

'Mrs Neufelt?' one asked.

'No I'm Mr Neufelt's partner. Mr Neufelt's not in at the moment. Can I help?' she asked apprehensively.

'Can you confirm that Mr Neufelt was flying on State Airlines flight 413?' asked the policeman reading from a book.

Pamela's hand went to her mouth as she took a deep breath and gasped 'Oh!'. Then she continued 'He was flying today but I can't confirm the flight number'.

'I'm afraid that the flight has crashed.'

Pamela screamed and cried towards the ceiling 'No, please God, No, not Simon'.

'I have to say that the search is continuing' one policeman said in a soft sympathetic voice.

She sank slowly to her knees sobbing, her body shaking violently.

Both policemen stepped forward and helped her to a chair. One stepped out to the car and radioed for help from social services.

The sound of tyres on gravel grabbed their attention. This was followed by a knock at the kitchen door. Pamela's head raised from the table where it had been resting and she pointed at the door asking in a muffled voice, directed at the policeman, 'Would you answer that?'

A female came through the opening and produced an ID to the senior policeman who in response said 'Miss Fry, can I outline the circumstances?' as he beckoned her outside again.

After a few moments the two returned and stood at the table where Pamela's head was still resting on her arms. The senior man spoke gently to Pamela.

'Excuse me madam.' Pamela's head came up.

'Yes?' she mumbled displaying bleary eyes.

'This is Miss Fry. She's here to comfort you and she will stay with you until you both feel she may go. My partner and I have to leave now so I'll say goodbye.' The policemen left.

After a moment or two, Pamela raised her head from the table and looked at the other woman.

'Miss Fry?' she asked frowning, 'Miss Sheila Fry?'

'That's me' Miss Fry answered.

The two women scanned each other's faces. Gradually, a look of recognition brightened Sheila's serious countenance. 'You're Pamela Shelby' she announced.

'You're correct' Pamela shouted smiling and then stood up. The two women embraced and kissed affectionately. Eventually Pamela stepped back her arms on Sheila's shoulders. 'Let me take a look at you' she said. 'You look wonderful!' Pamela smiled as they embraced again. Holding hands Pamela led the way out of the kitchen along the short corridor into the bedroom where she threw herself onto the bed pulling Sheila down with her.

Looking into Sheila's eyes she said 'Sheila, I am so miserable. It's fortuitous you should come when you did, you have made my day. I'm so pleased to see you'.

'I'm happy to see you too Pamela.' They kissed.

'After all these years' Pamela sighed.

Sheila asked 'So what's been happening Pam?'

Pamela ran through her recent history and completed with Simon's plane crash and suspected death. She referred to the book and her hatred of it.

The two met as toddlers when the parents were neighbours and parted when their parents moved away in different directions. They met up again at university both studying psychology.

Sheila said 'Pamela, I'm surprised that you could allow a book to influence your prejudice'.

'I can assure you that this book is quite capable. It's responsible for the deaths of eight people.'

'You don't think that a hidden prejudice against your father is surfacing via his belongings, because of his abuse of you?' Sheila asked averting her eyes.

'Sheila, I never thought my father abused me. Did you know he was my stepfather by the way?'

'Yes I do know, you told me years ago.'

'I loved my father Sheila.'

Pamela rolled over onto her back and looking up at the ceiling said as if to herself, 'That book has been responsible for all those deaths and now Simon's'. Tears began forming in her eyes. 'Is there no end to it?'

Sheila studied Pamela's face. 'Do you still think about your father now' she asked.

'All the time' came the answer. 'He is the standard by which I measure all other men.'

'What were your feelings toward him when he was alive?'

'I had a deep love for him. He was so gentle and kind. He bought all my clothes and everything I needed. I seldom asked for anything because I never needed anything. He would suggest that I had something and the next day I would have it and I always found his presents wonderful. He was kind and thoughtful and I was happy to do anything he asked.

'My mother married him when my real father died and then when I was aged seven she died. From then on my stepfather did everything for me. He fed me dressed me and bathed me. We did everything together. We shared the bath and shared the bed from the very first day and I was never happy without him. He cared for me in every way and constantly demonstrated his love for me in word and deed. When you came to visit and we shared a bed I enjoyed being with you but I always felt that I was shutting my father out' she said wistfully.

'You know, all the girls had a crush on him. I did' said Sheila. She now was also talking to the ceiling. 'How old were you when he first penetrated you?' There was a long pause. Both women continued to look at the ceiling.

'I was twelve' answered Pamela.

'What were the circumstances?'

'It was during the oil massage after the bath. I was on all fours and he was massaging my back.'

'What were your feelings during and afterwards?'

'I was quite comfortable with it. I just accepted it as a natural sequence of events. You see I had grown used to the finger prodding every night in the bath and he was so gentle, he never hurt me.

'Whenever he was alone with another woman I always felt jealous. I even felt jealous when you were with him sometimes, but not always.'

Pamela was aware that Sheila had slept with her father on many occasions when they were at university but she had a deep affection for her friend and didn't regard her as a threat since they were sometimes all in the bed together.

Sheila was deep in thought and they were silent for some time. She had formed the opinion that jealousy had taken a deep place in Pamela's emotions and placing her father on a pedestal as she had she made him her role model that no man was going to measure up to. She was surprised at her affection for Simon. It was so deep.

The two women slept solidly all night and in the morning they awoke to a glorious morning with sunshine beating through the big window. Pamela jumped out of bed and went through to the bathroom saying 'I'll take a shower'.

Sheila watched her leave through bleary eyes as she slowly forced her eyes open to accept the strong sunlight and promptly went into deep thought.

Within minutes Pamela came back to the bedroom and stopped and looked out of the window. Sheila looked at her standing naked in the bright sunlight and thought how beautiful she remained. Twenty years had passed since they last met yet she retained her youthful figure and looked just as lovely as she did then.

Sheila jumped up and headed for the bathroom passing Pamela at the window on the way. She stopped kissed Pamela and said 'I'll shower too' smiled and off she went.

When she returned she too stopped at the window to take in the view and turning, saw that Pamela was back in bed. Pamela stretched out an arm and said, in a husky voice, 'Come back to bed'. Sheila stepped over to the bed and lifted the covers and climbed in.

They lay there looking at the ceiling. Sheila said 'I must say, when we were young girls we had really happy times with your stepfather'.

'Yes' said Pamela wistfully.

'I remember the oil massage' Sheila said laughing. 'There was lots of tickling and giggling.'

'Yes. I enjoyed every moment of my childhood with you' Pamela sighed.

Sheila rolled over on to her side to face Pamela. Her hand gently stroked Pamela's face and they kissed. Their hands moved to caress each other's bodies and they kissed again, hungrily. Sheila stopped and stared at Pam, her mouth slightly open.

'All those years' she said softly. 'We could have been together all those years.'

They cuddled each other warmly.

'You look just as lovely as you did then' Pamela smiled as she wrapped her leg around Sheila's.

'And so do you' Sheila responded as she wriggled closer to Pamela.

Over the evening meal Sheila asked 'How did you meet Cynthia?'

'Her husband was the architect who designed my house and he introduced us when I told him I was interested in riding lessons. She gave me lessons and she was very good. She has always stabled her horses over at Mary's stables.'

Two days passed and Sheila was of the opinion that Pamela's condition had stabilised. It was therefore safe for her to leave and attend to her other work.

'Pamela, do you mind if I leave you for a couple of days?'

'Of course I don't. I realise you have your work to do dear. You do realise of course that I have to leave this house don't you?'

'No why?'

'Well this is not my house. I have my own home to go back to and it is better that you don't stay here because there may be danger here for you.'

'What do you mean danger?'

'I mean that I'm afraid for you. Everyone around me has died. I've lost everyone who was close to me and you mean a lot to me. I give off bad vibes.'

'You mean that damned book?'

Pamela was silent for a moment.

'Yes I mean that damned book. That book has left its vibes in this house and the sooner we're both out of it the better.'

'Oh Pamela don't be so stupid. I refuse to accept such a silly assumption. I agree that you must leave here but you can stay at my place. Yes, I agree that it's a good thing that you cut all connection with this house but for other reasons. Yes leave this house, I'm comfortable with that. Check out your own house and then come to stay with me. How's that?'

'That's fine. You attend to your work and I'll speak to you in a couple of days.'

Sheila packed her bag and left.

A couple of days passed and Pamela had heard no news of Simon. She concluded that he must be dead although she continued to think of him and their times together. She hadn't known him a great length of time but the time they had was so rich in happiness and genuine affection. These thoughts fostered a general mood of depression and led her to drinking. She could not possibly concentrate on her work. She considered other ways of occupying her mind.

She would go horse riding. She phoned the stable to arrange a suitable time then drove down on a fine clear morning. At the stable she pulled into the parking lot and walked over to the office where she found Mary engrossed in paperwork.

As she entered Mary stood up and screeched 'Pamela!' and they embraced. 'What a surprise' she continued, 'and you don't look well'.

'Simon is dead' Pam said.

'What?' Mary's eyes popped open to twice their normal size as she pushed a fist into her mouth.

Pamela told her the full story as their eyes filled with tears and Pam's voice choked out the words.

The two women comforted each other as question and answer passed back and forth. Mary said 'What a terrible way to die. We'll sue the goddamn airline.'

'I loved him you know but I only found out when it was too late' Pamela spoke into her handkerchief.

'I'm not surprised, he was such a nice chap Pam.'

Two young riders passed the window at a slow canter and stopped at the open office door.

Mary said 'Would you excuse me Pam? I have a lesson which will take around thirty minutes, I'm sorry dear. Make yourself a cup of tea.'

'Of course' Pam replied as Mary left the office. She watched as Mary spoke to the young riders outside and then climbed onto her own horse tied up at the hitching rail. She led the three at a slow walk out of the yard into the covered arena with a sand covered floor.

Pamela watched in a distant, disorientated way through the window as the teenagers went through the initial stages of their lesson. Mary was standing in the centre of a circle as the girls walked round her as she called instructions in a loud clear voice.

Suddenly another stable girl came into the office. 'Are you riding this morning?' she asked.

Pamela was surprised by the intrusion. 'Oh ... er ... yes.'

'You ride Dover don't you?'

'Yes.'

'I'll saddle him up for you.'

'Thank you.'

As she sat there in the office, her vacant mind was suddenly presented with vivid pictures. Pictures of Simon sitting in a snow covered landscape surrounded by a mass of jagged metal that was the remains of a disintegrated plane. She heard him moan in pain and she whimpered and squeezed her thighs together as her eyes filled with tears.

She sat stiffly upright, staring out front vacantly trying to shut out the events being re-enacted in her mind. She didn't know the manner of his death, she could only imagine the agony that one experiences in a plane crash. She saw his body damaged and covered in blood. Her hands went up to her face in an attempt to smother the pictures that seemed so real. She sobbed into her handkerchief quietly alone, in the silence of the office.

The stable girl called from the yard to say that the horse was ready. She stood up, brushed herself down and walked to where the horse was standing patiently with his nose being stroked by the young handler.

Pamela mounted and walked sedately out of the yard, oblivious of everything and everyone around her. She walked out into the open country and on into the wooded area that she rode with Simon. She recalled that one and only visit that Simon made to the stable when they rode out together on a day much like this one.

Mary completed the lesson and returned to the yard. Passing through the paddock she scanned the area quickly and walked into the office. She saw Pam's handbag on the desk and tidied the paperwork that was scattered over the top that she was working on when Pam arrived. She decide to finish it while she was waiting for Pam to come back.

The two riders came back from the arena where she had left them to practise what they had learned. She went out to inspect the horses. They were neighing and shaking their heads but they were looking good. She handed the two animals over to the stable girl and returned to the paperwork bidding the young riders goodbye.

Two hours had passed and she began to worry. The temperature was dropping.

She scanned the horizon from her office window. Turning to the hatchway in the partition at the side of her desk she opened it and called through to the stable girl, 'Lucy will you saddle my horse again?'

Mary had decided to go out and look for Pamela. She appreciated the gravity of the mental state she was in and she didn't like the way she looked and sounded before she went out. Lucy brought the horse to the door and Mary went out and mounted straightaway galloping out of the yard.

After an hour of searching she found no sign of her. Now she was seriously worried. She began listing the possible things she might have done. Places she might have gone. She'd never seen her in this condition before. The situation could be serious. She searched all the known places that might be used as a hiding place.

The light was fading and that wouldn't help a prolonged search. She stopped her horse and listened for any distant sound and as she did so it occurred to her that there must be something else bothering Pamela. Something more than Simon's death. The strange thing is that she had always suspected that Pamela was a lesbian and for her to have such a deep feeling for a male just didn't fit.

She increased her speed to a gallop to cover ground further out. Suddenly she saw a figure in the distance. In the dusk light she saw her. It was Pamela. She was standing by a pool giving the horse a drink. She galloped over to her, reducing to a trot as she approached.

She called 'Pamela, Hi!'

Pamela turned and waved in an unenthusiastic way.

Mary saw the way that Pamela looked at her. She looked as if the floodgates of her misery would open up again. There was a slight indication of relief at the corners of her mouth as if she was glad to have someone she could at last share the anguish and pain she had endured mentally whilst alone for the last few hours.

As the two horses touched sides Pauline's hand reached up to Mary. Her eyes were surrounded in dark rings and the lids were red and wet. Mary reached her arm down and placed it around Pamela's shoulder in a small measure of reassurance. Leaning down she said gently 'Mount up and let's go back'.

Their horses walked slowly back to the yard neither woman said a word. They got back and unsaddled, fed and watered the animals, the stable girl had gone, then went into the flat.

Mary made tea and they sat in silence for a while. Suddenly Pamela said 'I saw a bear this afternoon, so did Dover and he bolted. He took me for miles.'

'I'm not surprised. Poor old Dover. I'm afraid we have seen bears around here lately. Are you all right?'

'Oh yes, I'm all right I was more worried about Dover but he settled down.

Mary looked into Pamela's eyes. She decided that the girl needed an interest. She said 'I need an assistant in the stables Pamela. Is that something you could take on?'

'Oh well I don't know. Is it something you think I could do?'

'I would say that you were admirably suited.'

'I would have to work it between my patients' appointments of course and if that's convenient I'd love to do it.'

'Good! When would you like to start?'

'Er ... well tomorrow I suppose.'

'Good, I'm so pleased. Drink your tea. Would you like something to eat?' Mary stood up and looked down at Pamela who now had the suggestion of a smile on her face.

'Yes I do believe I could eat a little something' she said.

'Good. Give me five minutes to shower and I'll see what we've got' Mary said as she skipped out of the room.

Pamela stood, took off her jacket and hung it on the hook behind the door. She walked over to the window and looked out at the stable yard, deep in thought.

Mary came back into the room, showered and dressed in clean clothes. 'Shower if you wish Pam' she said.

'Yes I will' Pamela replied and left the room leaving Mary to find some food.

They sat and ate and Mary was glad to see that Pamela had perked up no end.

'You'll stay tonight' Mary suggested.

'Yes I'll stay tonight' Pamela responded. 'Then I won't be late in the morning.'

In the morning Mary came back from the shower, knocked on Pamela's door and called 'Breakfast Pam' and returned to her own room to dress.

Dressed, she stepped back into the passage and called Pam again. Receiving no answer she knocked on the door and called her name again. Still no reply she knocked again and called again. She grabbed the door handle and, hesitating for a second she turned the knob and pushed the door open. She stood in the opening staring at the bed under the window and called Pamela's name. 'Pamela?'

Pamela was lying in bed as if asleep. Mary walked over to the divan looking down at her. Pam's complexion was the colour of uncooked pastry. By the bed stood a chair on which was a screw topped jar.

Mary didn't need to be told that her friend was dead. As she looked down at the body she felt as if she had been punched in the stomach. Mary whispered reverently 'Why Pam why?'

Grief came upon her in delayed shock and her eyes filled silently with tears. 'I knew you were unhappy Pam but this ...'

She turned and looked around the room wistfully as if searching for a reason. Pamela's clothes were placed tidily on a chair and she'd gone to bed in a nightdress that Mary had given her to wear. Mary's gaze returned to the bedside chair. She looked closely at the screw top jar. It contained sleeping pills.

Mary's hand went to her open mouth to mask a sharp intake of breath.

Professor Grayden was a gentle person, very thoughtful and kind. The front part of his head was bald and always had been as far back as anyone could remember. People said that the baldness was brought about by the worry he undertook on behalf of his patients.

He was a psychologist and his workload was enormous. His office had psychics ringing every day giving their advice about the bells ringing in their own ears.

The professor spoke perfect English with the touch of an accent. This made an instant impression on a patient. Few things were more persuasive than an expert with an accent and a foreign name. He had noticed that few private patients objected to the unbelievably high cost of his treatment sessions.

At the moment, he was very concerned with Pamela. He had been worried about her since her last visit to him. She was a self employed psychologist and she worked for him by attending to those patients that he could not deal with. His workload was so big lately that he was having to pass more and more over to her.

He was worried that he might be the cause of the pressure that she appeared to be under. Her last visit was to bring in the reports of her recent work. She looked very ill and depressed. He recalled that her father in his last days was unbalanced, that was not a good sign.

Pamela looked exceedingly unhappy during that last meeting. He picked up his horn-rimmed glasses from his desktop and opened the arms pushing the end of one between his lips. Pondering deeply he forced thoughts to drift through his memory dragging them up from the basement of his mind.

What could be the cause of her depression? He thought of the patients in his hospital and the patterns of depression they presented. He and Pamela had been friends for years and he was genuinely concerned for her. She had come to work for him ten years ago and he was immediately impressed by her work. Since then he had learned to trust her judgement.

He considered the peculiar way some of his patients in the hospital looked at situations and how they dealt with things. He knew that everyone had a signature. He now had to identify Pamela's signature.

He began listing her possible problems. One, she was lonely. He

The Illusive Diamond

recalled that he had never known her to have a man friend. She was lonely and eager, a frightened and angry young woman. A young woman looking for love. She gave the impression lately of being lost. Of being irritated and uncomfortable. Strange, he thought. Very strange. He must give her a break. He would advise her to take a holiday. He would contact her today and he would immediately reduce her workload. She was decidedly suicidal.

He looked around his room. It had a kind of cluttered emptiness with books everywhere interspersed with files and papers. Bookshelves lined the walls and there were little piles of books around the floor.

The fact that he could not recall her ever having had a man friend might mean that she had a problem identifying her own sexuality. This alone could be devastating. She was not an alcoholic, which was a good sign, since that was usually the route taken by people searching for a meaning to their life. The two usually came together.

The professor had met the result of alcohol abuse during his army service. Just after the end of World War II he left college with a degree in psychology and was called into the Army to treat traumatised soldiers. He was sent to the British zone of Germany to join the Military Police to assist in the searches that were going on to find and identify escaped Nazis, some of whom had joined the bands of displaced persons wandering Germany. These hated monsters took refuge in any way they could, particularly among the ordinary folk of Germany, losing themselves among the workers and normal life. Attempting to become part of a community working as farmers or labourers, hiding within the life of the village.

Most of the time the villagers recognised them for what they were, by their bearing and attitude. As much as they tried to conceal their background it was impossible. They were left on the outside of things.

Professor Grayden was placed in charge of a squad of military policemen travelling round the German villages hunting for Nazis in hiding. His plan was simple. He would ask the villagers straight out: were there any Nazis in the village? The pattern was the same. The squad would walk into a village and call the inhabitants together. The village was combed to be sure everyone was there and then the question was put to them.

No answer was forthcoming. The faces were scanned. Any guilty looking faces were taken away and questioned. Doubtful answers were dealt with instantly. The man was shot on the spot.

After a day's work in this squad the men spent the night in the bar and got legless and as time went by the men became useless at that job or any other job. Killing Nazis was pleasurable in the beginning but teams had to change frequently because shooting a man at point blank range was not an easy task for civilised men. Alcohol was a refuge for the moment but was not a permanent remedy.

The professor reflected on this as he absently scanned the notes on his desk. His thoughts returned to the last time he saw Pamela. She was upset and her face was hopelessly tired. He thought she was concealing some kind of secret misery. He had to find the causal relationship for her present mental condition.

He idly picked up the phone and called the clinic to see if there were any messages. He took notes as the long list was dictated then straightened up in his chair as the last message was recited. Then suddenly he raised his eyebrows when he heard the last word.

Pamela had not kept an appointment at the clinic today. She had been found dead in bed this morning.

CHAPTER 15

The body of the plane shook violently as the airframe shuddered under the strain of the demands placed upon it. The engines screamed as they clawed the air in an effort to answer the requirements of the pilot who asked the plane to stand on its tail.

The captain rolled the plane to the left then to the right struggling against the updraft in an effort to avoid the cornice that had appeared in his path.

The mist had cleared suddenly and the top of the mountain had appeared before him in brilliant sunshine. He could miss the shelf below the cornice but ... the cornice was huge.

The plane was being drawn into the giant overhang. The captain's face was taut. He spoke to the passengers' cabin over the intercom, 'Will you ensure that your safety belt is on and will you please bend forward placing your head between your knees, clasping your hands behind your neck, thank you'.

The strange thing is, that one second after the initial impact, when the pilot, who was strapped to his seat was thrown into the folding nose as it crunched into the rock face, there was complete silence.

The layer of snow had deadened the sound of metal crashing against the mountain in the first instance but human sounds were non existent one second after bodies had passed through the meat grinder of flying metal and missiles through the length of the cabin. Accompanied by screams and crashings they covered the distance in about one minute before meeting their final second on this earth at the mountainside in total silence.

At the moment of impact, the two people behind Simon were

thrown over his head and wedged momentarily across his lap until the seat in front of him collapsed, allowing them to continue their flight towards the front. This took something in the order of three seconds, sufficient to slow his journey and make him the last to travel forward.

The front of the plane collapsed on impact and people and things were catapulted into the nose where the captain and his crew had been sitting, then on into the ice of the mountain.

On the way most had been scythed by chards of metal slicing the air, having been ripped from the position for which they were designed.

For one moment shouts and screams filled the air with the sound of tearing metal along with the thud of bodies colliding with each other and pieces of furniture and fuselage.

Simon was thrown forward, still strapped to his seat, the fixing having given way. The person who fell across him had slowed his progress forward until that side of the fuselage had disintegrated, throwing him free through the huge gap torn in the side. He was thrown sideways in a head roll strapped to the seat striking the mountainside, seat first, in deep snow at forty five degrees to the crash site where everyone else had been thrown to their death. He suffered a whiplash rendering him unconscious.

The packed snow into which he fell immediately began to move taking him and his seat with it. Gradually the seat picked up speed as, cutting through the snow, it skated on the substrate ice on the increasingly steep slope.

Eventually, the angle of descent reduced and the chair struck deep snow again. As the speed reduced the chair dug deep into the soft snow and stopped five feet down. As the chair buried itself, the snow fell in behind it and covered its tracks. Simon was buried there for twenty four hours on the blind side of the mountain.

When he regained consciousness he found himself in a cave of snow still strapped to the seat. The upholstery had protected him from frostbite and retained his body heat. A small hole, left in the crumbling snow that followed the chair, maintained air flow.

He released the safety belt on the seat and pushed his hand above his head making a hole quite easily in the soft snow through which he was able to see clear sky. He stood shakily to his feet pushing his head and shoulders up through the snow. As his head cleared the snowline he saw clear blue sky and a peaceful white landscape. The storm had passed and all was still.

The Illusive Diamond

It took some time for him to release his arms and legs that were stiff with the cold and lack of use, but eventually he climbed up on the back of the chair and pulled himself out of the hole in the snow. He was instantly struck by the drop in the temperature comparing it with the hole in the snow which was quite snug by comparison.

His eyes struggled against the glare of the snow as he scanned the foreground and he had to cover his eyes for a moment as he accustomed himself to the brightness. He moved his forearm across his face to protect his eyes and lost his balance falling back into the snow.

He was presented by pictures of a dream-like quality that closed in on him in real time dimension. It was actually happening to him now. He was in a shootout situation with two other men, one of them was Mark. Simon had fired and killed Mark and had to bury him quickly because of the danger of wolves that were on the prowl.

There was a dead girl being raped in the background. Simon shot the man who was doing the raping. There was guitar music in the background playing somewhere in the distance.

Voices purveyed the whole scene. A deep male voice was offering him advice that he should not marry while a pleasant female voice was begging him to marry her. The mass of sound was defused by a high wind and the panoramic scene was defused by snowflakes falling gently softening the sound of screaming females completing a picture of total chaos.

He was rushing to bury Mark because the wolves were closing in and Mark's wound was bleeding. The burial had to be completed before the animals appeared. The wolves were now very close and Simon was digging like mad. The ground was very hard and it was frustrating to make such little progress. He was sweating in the freezing atmosphere. He must get this done. He must get this done. The wolves were here, they were growling and slobbering. The leading animal jumped at Simon. He reached for his gun as the slobbering animal landed on him. He emptied the chamber into the mass of fur as he fell backwards into a shallow ditch.

He thrashed around for a time but seemed to make matters worse as he got deeper in the snow. He rolled over and over in the soft fluffy snow trying to get to his feet. Finally he found a reasonably solid surface which allowed him to stand upright. He scrambled to his feet and shielding his eyes he began once again searching the horizon.

He saw a rocky outcrop and walked over to it. Sitting down on it he continued scanning the far distance on both sides of his position and below him.

After what seemed an age he thought he saw movement on the horizon. He studied the area and eventually was convinced of his suspicion, they were moving across his front. He waved frantically for some time in an effort to gain their attention.

Just when he thought he was wasting his time he stopped waving, despondent and shoulders aching, he saw them change their direction and begin moving towards him. They had spotted him. He collapsed onto the snow. From that moment he remembered nothing.

He was slipping in and out of consciousness and was aware of the swish of metal sliding on snow and he seemed to be suspended in space. He could hear strange voices and he could smell an animal scent which seemed strangely familiar. He was aware of the sensation of rocking from side to side and he also had the feeling of being strapped down.

He was overtaken by panic as he seemed to be slipping into a black hole. Was he still in the aeroplane? He wanted to scream 'WHERE THE HELL AM I?'

He awoke to a rocking motion. There was a sound of snorting and snuffling and there was the sound of clanging of a little bell. The air was heavy with an acrid animal smell. He was subjected to a rhythmic movement. There was a padding of feet, the swishing of snow.

He had been here before. Where was he? The whole process seemed familiar. The swishing, the dull plodding, the clanging, the gentle rhythm and the kind of muffled silence.

He began to hallucinate. His head began to ache. He was no longer part of this scene. He felt terribly weak and was slipping into unconsciousness, he gladly surrendered to the feeling being totally disorientated and having no connection with reality.

He was falling into a huge chasm with no bottom. Blackness had descended and he was drifting into space. Perhaps he was dying. So this was what death was like! The rocking movement overtook him and he slipped into deep unconsciousness.

The gentle motion created a sensation that shook pictures from his mind. Pictures of his recent past. He was lying in the snow but he couldn't see Mark's body. What happened to Mark's body? He was reminded that he hadn't buried Mark. Had the wolves got him? He was reminded that he hadn't caught up with Mark's killer. He was suddenly steeped in an overpowering depression.

The Illusive Diamond

He was drowning in a kaleidoscope of moving colours. He saw the pilot of the plane wrestling with the controls. He saw people flying past him shouting and screaming. Bags and cases joined the space race with the bodies all heading in the same direction. The air was filled with sediment absorbing the natural daylight. He was cautiously making his way towards an opening through which daylight appeared to be forcing its way.

His breathing was loud and his heart was pounding as he tried to control his breathing. His movements were laboured as he fought his way through the mass of flying jumble. He stopped for a moment and held on to a seat back, closing his eyes.

Something struck him in the middle of his back. He let go of the seatback and allowed himself to float freely towards the opening from where the daylight was coming. He looked around for recognisable features but through the murkiness could only make out vague shapes. The colours were becoming more vibrant now and he shielded his eyes from the effect. He was being driven along by a wind of unbelievable pressure creating its own ghostly whine.

He wrapped his arms around his head in protection against flying objects.

He was back in the plane and a wind was shaking the fuselage as it rushed around the interior making a screaming sound like ghosts in pain. Blood rushed to his head making his eyes ache. He was trembling. His mind tried to control his anguish. He was being overcome by his emotions.

The sky was a dark gunmetal grey splashed with streaks of orange copper. A book flew past him. It was THE ILLUSIVE DIAMOND.

He remembered that all the students had a copy. In fact he observed that distribution of the book must have reached saturation point. It was a pity that everyone who read the book ... My God! Can that be true? Everyone who read the book had died?

It was night and the moon was full and bright. Simon looked around. A herd of deer lay motionless in the snow. There was a small tent erected a short distance from him and he could hear low voices coming from it.

He lay there strapped down and he inspected the straps and his covering. The straps were leather and the covering was hide and very warm. He heard a crunching in the snow and looked towards the sound. A man was approaching from the tent. He was dressed in the same hide as that covering Simon. Obviously Innuit, he stepped up beside Simon and looked down at him. Innuit are not renowned for their brilliance but they are very well known for their amazing memory.

Simon looked up at him. A faint look of recognition passed between the two. The man spoke.

'You are Simon.'

Simon frowned in disbelief. 'How do you know that?' he asked.

'Because I keep finding you in the snow.'

'You do?'

'Twenty years ago I found you in the snow at Fort Franklin with a bullet in you and I took you to the Legat Mine. I thought that was the last I would see of you but I couldn't speak English then.'

END

Printed in the United Kingdom
by Lightning Source UK Ltd.
101992UKS00001B/175